博雅 英语专业博雅教育课程系列教材

荷马史诗
奥德赛选读

王珊珊 主编

SELECTED
READINGS OF
THE ODYSSEY

清华大学出版社
北 京

内 容 简 介

本教材是对《奥德赛》的节选、导读、注释和讨论。全书分十二章，每章均包含导读、选文和思考题三个部分，每章选文均取自《奥德赛》的著名篇章。本教材供英语专业本科生使用，有利于提升学生的人文素养，加深对史诗文学的理解与欣赏，了解古希腊的政治、经济、文化习俗。

图书在版编目（CIP）数据

荷马史诗奥德赛选读 / 王珊珊主编. —北京：清华大学出版社，2020. 6（2025.2重印）
英语专业博雅教育课程系列教材
ISBN 978-7-302-55238-3

Ⅰ. ①荷… Ⅱ. ①王… Ⅲ. ①史诗–古希腊–高等学校–教材 Ⅳ. ①I545.22
中国版本图书馆CIP数据核字（2020）第047882号

责任编辑：钱屹芝
封面设计：子 一
责任校对：王凤芝
责任印制：宋 林

出版发行：清华大学出版社
　　　　　网　　　址：https://www.tup.com.cn，https://www.wqxuetang.com
　　　　　地　　　址：北京清华大学学研大厦A座　　　邮　　编：100084
　　　　　社 总 机：010-83470000　　　邮　　购：010-62786544
　　　　　投稿与读者服务：010-62776969, c-service@tup.tsinghua.edu.cn
　　　　　质量反馈：010-62772015, zhiliang@tup.tsinghua.edu.cn
印 装 者：三河市铭诚印务有限公司
经　　销：全国新华书店
开　　本：185mm×260mm　　　印　　张：10.5　　字　　数：204千字
版　　次：2020 年 7 月第 1 版　　　印　　次：2025 年 2 月第 3 次印刷
定　　价：42.00元

产品编号：071836-01

前言 PREFACE

　　《奥德赛》的故事发生在《伊利亚特》之后。特洛伊战争之后，希腊英雄们各自返乡，有的成功回国，有的葬身大海，有的受尽磨难。《奥德赛》讲述的就是英雄奥德修斯在特洛伊战争后历尽艰险，十年后才返回家园的故事。

　　《伊利亚特》展现的是一个稳定的世界，而《奥德赛》展现的是一个变动的世界。在《伊利亚特》中，人物姓甚名谁都是清楚的，自己清楚，敌人清楚，朋友清楚，读者也清楚；而《奥德赛》中的主人公却总要掩饰自己的真实身份，如若不然就可能面临杀身之祸。《伊利亚特》的世界是有秩序的，主人公的目的是要破坏现存秩序；而《奥德赛》的世界是无秩序的，主人公的目的是要恢复旧有秩序。在有秩序的世界中，对抗是在规则之下进行的，如阿喀琉斯杀死赫克托耳是通过堂堂正正的比武决斗；而在无秩序的世界中，决定生死的斗争随时随地都会发生，考验的是一个人是否观察敏锐、行动迅速。通常的看法认为，这两部史诗侧重表现了英雄们的两种不同品质：《伊利亚特》表现的是勇力，《奥德赛》表现的是智力。在《奥德赛》中，奥德修斯的聪明才智虽然表现得淋漓尽致，但须知他经历的那众多磨难，没有强绝力量和毅力的人是不可能承受的：没有力量他就无法奋力划船，躲过海怪斯库拉的吞噬；没有力量他就不能在竞赛中打败费埃克斯人，赢得他们的尊敬和帮助；没有力量他就不可能拉开强弓射穿十二个斧孔，杀死求婚者，赢回本属于自己的家产、妻子和荣誉。

　　《伊利亚特》的结果是一个平衡的打破。特洛伊被攻陷之后，城市在烧杀抢掠下不复存在，幸存者各自苦苦寻觅生路，其中最著名的是埃涅阿斯历经千难万险来到意大利建城，最终成为罗马人祖先的故事。希腊英雄们也面临同样的问题，他们掠夺了战利品，各自踏上归程，旋即面临不同的命运：阿伽门农回家后即遭妻子及其情人的杀害；墨涅拉奥斯经历了八年海上历险才返回斯巴达；而奥德修斯的经历最为坎坷，在海上漂泊十载，回到伊塔卡后还要面对穷凶极恶的求婚者。回家，其实质就是要重建秩序，阿伽门农没能做到，奥德修斯做到了。奥德修斯被仙女卡吕普索囚禁的时候生活平静，他却不愿留下。魔女基尔克挽留奥德修斯一年，饱食终日，无忧无虑，最终他依然选择离开。《奥德赛》的主题就是回家，家的价值被置于所有价值之上，是主人公历尽千辛万苦的终极追求。家的价值体现在对家族传承的重视，对夫妻恩爱、家庭和美的向往，对家族财富的获取和积累传承等多方面。在史诗中很多著名情节都表现了这一价值，例如阿喀琉斯的灵魂对父亲和儿子消息的探寻、奥德修斯对费埃克斯国王和王后的祝福等。

《奥德赛》中充满了欺骗的言行，表现了英雄的聪颖狡狯。奥德修斯为了保全自己、击败敌人，有时使用假名，有时延缓透露真实身份，有时编造身世，有时乔装易服。体现出同样特性的也不止他一人，最典型的是他的妻子佩涅洛佩，为了拖延求婚人，她假装给尤利西斯的父亲做寿衣，白天缝，夜晚拆，寿衣永远做不好。求婚人就这样被骗了三年，直到佩涅洛佩被女仆出卖。即使面对自己的丈夫时，她也要使用唯有二人知晓的隐秘来试探验证，绝不肯轻易相信。奥德修斯的身份，在他的历险中经常要经历从隐瞒到显露的过程，每一次从隐瞒到显露的节奏都不相同，故事就是在这样相似的步骤、相异的节奏中逐渐展开，其结局也各不相同。

本书是对《奥德赛》的节选、导读、注释和讨论。经过几年的读书、教学，作者将自己对史诗的研习和理解汇编成教材。该教材供英语专业本科生使用，是学生进入西方经典学习的入门书，有助于提升学生的人文素养。这本教材对于没有开设古典学的高校尤其适合。全书分十二章，每章均包含导读、选文和思考题三个部分。每章选文均取自《奥德赛》的著名篇章，节选原文大约一卷或两卷的篇幅，作者对文中难点都酌情做了简要的注释。在每章的选文之前，作者做了简明的导读，概括正文的主要内容，提示需要重点阅读的部分，引导读者关注史诗文学的创作特点，以及古希腊的政治、经济、文化习俗。在选文之后精心设计了一些针对性很强的思考题，进一步帮助读者掌握选篇的主要内容，加深对史诗的文学手法的理解与欣赏。本书适合一学期授课量，教师可酌情安排进度。本书为中央财经大学外国语学院教材资助项目，在此表示感谢！

本书所选用的英语译本是 Samuel Butler 翻译的 *The Odyssey*。译本中的人物使用的是罗马名字，如主人公奥德修斯被翻译成尤利西斯，雅典娜为密涅瓦，等等。此译本为散文体，流畅可读，颇便于初学者。

王珊珊

2020 年 3 月

目录

第一章

众神会议 独子寻父

导读

INTRODUCTION

本章选自《奥德赛》第一卷。众神召集会议，决议让尤利西斯归返家园。密涅瓦随即幻化成门特斯来到尤利西斯的故乡伊塔卡，鼓励尤利西斯的儿子特勒马科斯鼓起勇气应对求婚者，并出海探寻父亲的消息。尤利西斯此时正受困于卡吕普索的岛屿，生死不为妻儿所知。在他的家中，强横的求婚者以向佩涅洛佩求婚为名，寻欢作乐，耗费他的家财。佩涅洛佩一介妇人，无力反抗。特勒马科斯刚刚成年，势单力薄，也不敢反抗，只能眼睁睁地看着家财被无赖的求婚者大肆耗费。

本章的开篇就涉及史诗的另一条故事线索，即尤利西斯的儿子特勒马科斯寻父，也包含了另一个故事主题：特勒马科斯的成长。读者须注意这条故事线索和这一故事主题与《奥德赛》全篇的故事主线和主题——回家的关系。

密涅瓦来到尤利西斯家中，受到特勒马科斯招待。本卷描写的希腊人的待客之道，是有关希腊人社交、风俗的重要材料，请读者特别留意。尤利西斯在历险中遇见过不同国家、民族的人，他们风俗各异，并不遵循希腊人的待客礼仪，读者在后几章中将会看到，可以留心做一个对比。

选文

SELECTION

Tell me, O Muse, of that ingenious hero who travelled far and wide after he had sacked the famous town of Troy. Many cities did he visit, and many were the nations with whose manners and customs he was acquainted; moreover he suffered much by sea while trying to save his own life and bring his men safely home; but do what he might he could not save his men, for they perished through their own sheer folly in eating the cattle of the Sun-god Hyperion; so the god prevented them from ever reaching home. Tell me, too, about all these things, oh daughter of Jove, from whatsoever source you may know them.

So now all who escaped death in battle or by shipwreck had got safely home except Ulysses, and he, though he was longing to return to his wife and country, was detained by the goddess Calypso, who had got him into a large cave and wanted to marry him. But as years went by, there came a time when the gods settled that he should go back to Ithaca; even then, however, when he was among his own people, his troubles were not yet over; nevertheless all the gods had now begun to pity him except Neptune, who still persecuted him without ceasing and would not let him get home.

Now Neptune had gone off to the Ethiopians, who are at the world's end, and lie in two halves, the one looking West and the other East. He had gone there to accept a hecatomb of sheep and oxen, and was enjoying himself at his festival; but the other gods met in the house of Olympian Jove, and the sire of gods and men spoke first. At that moment he was thinking of Aegisthus[1], who had been killed by Agamemnon's son Orestes; so he said to the other gods: "See now, how men lay blame upon us gods for what is after all nothing but their own folly. Look at Aegisthus; he must needs make love to Agamemnon's wife unrighteously and then kill Agamemnon, though he knew it would be the death of him; for I sent Mercury to warn him not to do either of these things, inasmuch as Orestes would be sure to take his revenge when he grew up and wanted to return home. Mercury told him this in all good will but he would not listen, and now he has paid for everything in full."

Then Minerva said, "Father, son of Saturn, King of kings, it served Aegisthus right, and so it would any one else who does as he did; but Aegisthus is neither here nor there; it is for Ulysses that my heart bleeds, when I think of his sufferings in that lonely sea-girt island, far away, poor man, from all his friends. It is an island covered with forest, in the very middle of the sea, and a goddess lives there, daughter of the magician Atlas, who looks after the bottom of the ocean, and carries the great columns that keep heaven and earth asunder. This daughter of Atlas has got hold of poor unhappy Ulysses, and keeps trying by every kind of blandishment to make him forget his home, so that he is tired of life, and thinks of nothing but how he may once more see the smoke of his own chimneys. You, sir, take no heed of this, and yet when Ulysses was before Troy did he not propitiate you with many a burnt sacrifice? Why then should you keep on being so angry with him?"

And Jove said, "My child, what are you talking about? How can I forget Ulysses than whom there is no more capable man on earth, nor more liberal in his offerings to the immortal gods that live in heaven? Bear in mind, however, that Neptune is still furious with Ulysses for having blinded an eye of Polyphemus king of the Cyclopes. Polyphemus is son to Neptune by the nymph Thoosa, daughter to the sea-king Phorcys; therefore though he will not kill Ulysses outright, he torments him by preventing him from getting home. Still, let us lay our heads together and see how we can help him to return; Neptune will then be pacified, for if we are all of a mind he can hardly stand out against us."

And Minerva said, "Father, son of Saturn, King of kings, if, then, the gods now mean that Ulysses should get home, we should first send Mercury to the Ogygian island to tell Calypso that we have made up our minds and that he is to return. In the meantime I will go to Ithaca, to put heart into Ulysses' son Telemachus; I will embolden him to call the

---

1 Aegisthus 是阿伽门农（Agamemnon）的堂兄弟。

Achaeans[1] in assembly, and speak out to the suitors of his mother Penelope, who persist in eating up any number of his sheep and oxen; I will also conduct him to Sparta and to Pylos[2], to see if he can hear anything about the return of his dear father—for this will make people speak well of him."

So saying she bound on her glittering golden sandals, imperishable, with which she can fly like the wind over land or sea; she grasped the redoubtable bronze-shod spear, so stout and sturdy and strong, wherewith she quells the ranks of heroes who have displeased her, and down she darted from the topmost summits of Olympus, whereon forthwith she was in Ithaca, at the gateway of Ulysses' house, disguised as a visitor, Mentes, chief of the Taphians, and she held a bronze spear in her hand. There she found the lordly suitors seated on hides of the oxen which they had killed and eaten, and playing draughts in front of the house. Men-servants and pages were bustling about to wait upon them, some mixing wine with water in the mixing-bowls[3], some cleaning down the tables with wet sponges and laying them out again, and some cutting up great quantities of meat.

Telemachus saw her long before any one else did. He was sitting moodily among the suitors thinking about his brave father, and how he would send them flying out of the house, if he were to come to his own again and be honoured as in days gone by. Thus brooding as he sat among them, he caught sight of Minerva and went straight to the gate, for he was vexed that a stranger should be kept waiting for admittance. He took her right hand in his own, and bade her give him her spear. "Welcome," said he, "to our house, and when you have partaken of food you shall tell us what you have come for."

He led the way as he spoke, and Minerva followed him. When they were within he took her spear and set it in the spear-stand against a strong bearing-post along with the many other spears of his unhappy father, and he conducted her to a richly decorated seat under which he threw a cloth of damask. There was a footstool also for her feet, and he set another seat near her for himself, away from the suitors, that she might not be annoyed while eating by their noise and insolence, and that he might ask her more freely about his father.

1　Achaeans 是希腊人的统称。

2　Sparta 和 Pylos 都是古希腊城邦，它们的首领分别是墨涅拉奥斯（Menelaus）和涅斯托尔（Nestor），二人曾与尤利西斯一起远征特洛伊。

3　古希腊人喝酒时要向酒里掺水。

A maid servant then brought them water in a beautiful golden ewer and poured it into a silver basin for them to wash their hands, and she drew a clean table beside them. An upper servant brought them bread, and offered them many good things of what there was in the house, the carver fetched them plates of all manner of meats and set cups of gold by their side, and a manservant brought them wine and poured it out for them.

Then the suitors came in and took their places on the benches and seats. Forthwith men servants poured water over their hands, maids went round with the bread-baskets, pages filled the mixing-bowls with wine and water, and they laid their hands upon the good things that were before them. As soon as they had had enough to eat and drink they wanted music and dancing, which are the crowning embellishments of a banquet, so a servant brought a lyre to Phemius, whom they compelled perforce to sing to them. As soon as he touched his lyre and began to sing Telemachus spoke low to Minerva, with his head close to hers that no man might hear.

"I hope, sir," said he, "that you will not be offended with what I am going to say. Singing comes cheap to those who do not pay for it, and all this is done at the cost of one whose bones lie rotting in some wilderness or grinding to powder in the surf. If these men were to see my father come back to Ithaca they would pray for longer legs rather than a longer purse, for money would not serve them; but he, alas, has fallen on an ill fate, and even when people do sometimes say that he is coming, we no longer heed them; we shall never see him again. And now, sir, tell me and tell me true, who you are and where you come from. Tell me of your town and parents, what manner of ship you came in, how your crew brought you to Ithaca, and of what nation they declared themselves to be—for you cannot have come by land. Tell me also truly, for I want to know, are you a stranger to this house, or have you been here in my father's time? In the old days we had many visitors for my father went about much himself."

And Minerva answered, "I will tell you truly and particularly all about it. I am Mentes, son of Anchialus, and I am King of the Taphians. I have come here with my ship and crew, on a voyage to men of a foreign tongue being bound for Temesa with a cargo of iron, and I shall bring back copper. As for my ship, it lies over yonder off the open country away from the town, in the harbour Rheithron under the wooded mountain Neritum. Our fathers were friends before us, as old Laertes[1] will tell you, if you will go and ask him. They say, however,

---

1 Laertes 是奥德修斯的父亲。

that he never comes to town now, and lives by himself in the country, faring hardly, with an old woman to look after him and get his dinner for him, when he comes in tired from pottering about his vineyard. They told me your father was at home again, and that was why I came, but it seems the gods are still keeping him back, for he is not dead yet not on the mainland. It is more likely he is on some sea-girt island in mid ocean, or a prisoner among savages who are detaining him against his will. I am no prophet, and know very little about omens, but I speak as it is borne in upon me from heaven, and assure you that he will not be away much longer; for he is a man of such resource that even though he were in chains of iron he would find some means of getting home again. But tell me, and tell me true, can Ulysses really have such a fine looking fellow for a son? You are indeed wonderfully like him about the head and eyes, for we were close friends before he set sail for Troy where the flower of all the Argives[1] went also. Since that time we have never either of us seen the other."

"My mother," answered Telemachus, "tells me I am son to Ulysses, but it is a wise child that knows his own father. Would that I were son to one who had grown old upon his own estates, for, since you ask me, there is no more ill-starred man under heaven than he who they tell me is my father."

And Minerva said, "There is no fear of your race dying out yet, while Penelope has such a fine son as you are. But tell me, and tell me true, what is the meaning of all this feasting, and who are these people? What is it all about? Have you some banquet, or is there a wedding in the family—for no one seems to be bringing any provisions of his own? And the guests—how atrociously they are behaving; what riot they make over the whole house; it is enough to disgust any respectable person who comes near them."

"Sir," said Telemachus, "as regards your question, so long as my father was here it was well with us and with the house, but the gods in their displeasure have willed it otherwise, and have hidden him away more closely than mortal man was ever yet hidden. I could have borne it better even though he were dead, if he had fallen with his men before Troy, or had died with friends around him when the days of his fighting were done; for then the Achaeans would have built a mound over his ashes, and I should myself have been heir to his renown; but now the storm-winds have spirited him away we know not whither; he is gone without leaving so much as a trace behind him, and I inherit nothing but dismay.

---

1 Argives 指的是希腊人。

Nor does the matter end simply with grief for the loss of my father; heaven has laid sorrows upon me of yet another kind; for the chiefs from all our islands, Dulichium, Same, and the woodland island of Zacynthus, as also all the principal men of Ithaca itself, are eating up my house under the pretext of paying their court to my mother, who will neither point blank say that she will not marry, nor yet bring matters to an end; so they are making havoc of my estate, and before long will do so also with myself."

"Is that so?" exclaimed Minerva, "then you do indeed want Ulysses home again. Give him his helmet, shield, and a couple of lances, and if he is the man he was when I first knew him in our house, drinking and making merry, he would soon lay his hands about these rascally suitors, were he to stand once more upon his own threshold. He was then coming from Ephyra, where he had been to beg poison for his arrows from Ilus, son of Mermerus. Ilus feared the ever-living gods and would not give him any, but my father let him have some, for he was very fond of him. If Ulysses is the man he then was these suitors will have a short shrift and a sorry wedding.

"But there! It rests with heaven to determine whether he is to return, and take his revenge in his own house or no; I would, however, urge you to set about trying to get rid of these suitors at once. Take my advice, call the Achaean heroes in assembly to-morrow morning—lay your case before them, and call heaven to bear you witness. Bid the suitors take themselves off, each to his own place, and if your mother's mind is set on marrying again, let her go back to her father, who will find her a husband and provide her with all the marriage gifts that so dear a daughter may expect. As for yourself, let me prevail upon you to take the best ship you can get, with a crew of twenty men, and go in quest of your father who has so long been missing. Some one may tell you something, or (and people often hear things in this way) some heaven-sent message may direct you. First go to Pylos and ask Nestor; thence go on to Sparta and visit Menelaus, for he got home last of all the Achaeans; if you hear that your father is alive and on his way home, you can put up with the waste these suitors will make for yet another twelve months. If on the other hand you hear of his death, come home at once, celebrate his funeral rites with all due pomp, build a barrow to his memory, and make your mother marry again. Then, having done all this, think it well over in your mind how, by fair means or foul, you may kill these suitors in your own house. You are too old to plead infancy any longer; have you not heard how people are singing Orestes' praises for having killed his father's murderer Aegisthus? You are a fine, smart looking fellow; show your mettle, then, and make yourself a name in story. Now, however, I must go back to my ship and to my crew, who will be impatient if I keep them waiting longer; think the matter over for yourself, and remember what I have said to you."

"Sir," answered Telemachus, "it has been very kind of you to talk to me in this way, as though I were your own son, and I will do all you tell me; I know you want to be getting on with your voyage, but stay a little longer till you have taken a bath and refreshed yourself. I will then give you a present, and you shall go on your way rejoicing; I will give you one of great beauty and value—a keepsake such as only dear friends give to one another."

Minerva answered, "Do not try to keep me, for I would be on my way at once. As for any present you may be disposed to make me, keep it till I come again, and I will take it home with me. You shall give me a very good one, and I will give you one of no less value in return."

With these words she flew away like a bird into the air, but she had given Telemachus courage, and had made him think more than ever about his father. He felt the change, wondered at it, and knew that the stranger had been a god, so he went straight to where the suitors were sitting.

Phemius was still singing, and his hearers sat rapt in silence as he told the sad tale of the return from Troy, and the ills Minerva had laid upon the Achaeans. Penelope, daughter of Icarius, heard his song from her room upstairs, and came down by the great staircase, not alone, but attended by two of her handmaids. When she reached the suitors she stood by one of the bearing posts that supported the roof of the cloisters with a staid maiden on either side of her. She held a veil, moreover, before her face, and was weeping bitterly.

"Phemius," she cried, "you know many another feat of gods and heroes, such as poets love to celebrate. Sing the suitors some one of these, and let them drink their wine in silence, but cease this sad tale, for it breaks my sorrowful heart, and reminds me of my lost husband whom I mourn ever without ceasing, and whose name was great over all Hellas[1] and middle Argos[2]."

"Mother," answered Telemachus, "let the bard sing what he has a mind to; bards do not

---

1　Hellas 指的是古希腊。

2　Argos 地处希腊。

make the ills they sing of; it is Jove, not they, who makes them, and who sends weal or woe upon mankind according to his own good pleasure. This fellow means no harm by singing the ill-fated return of the Danaans[1], for people always applaud the latest songs most warmly. Make up your mind to it and bear it; Ulysses is not the only man who never came back from Troy, but many another went down as well as he. Go, then, within the house and busy yourself with your daily duties, your loom, your distaff, and the ordering of your servants; for speech is man's matter, and mine above all others—for it is I who am master here."

She went wondering back into the house, and laid her son's saying in her heart. Then, going upstairs with her handmaids into her room, she mourned her dear husband till Minerva shed sweet sleep over her eyes. But the suitors were clamorous throughout the covered cloisters, and prayed each one that he might be her bed fellow.

Then Telemachus spoke, "Shameless," he cried, "and insolent suitors, let us feast at our pleasure now, and let there be no brawling, for it is a rare thing to hear a man with such a divine voice as Phemius has; but in the morning meet me in full assembly that I may give you formal notice to depart, and feast at one another's houses, turn and turn about, at your own cost. If on the other hand you choose to persist in sponging upon one man, heaven help me, but Jove shall reckon with you in full, and when you fall in my father's house there shall be no man to avenge you."

The suitors bit their lips as they heard him, and marvelled at the boldness of his speech. Then, Antinous, son of Eupeithes, said, "The gods seem to have given you lessons in bluster and tall talking; may Jove never grant you to be chief in Ithaca as your father was before you."

Telemachus answered, "Antinous, do not chide with me, but, god willing, I will be chief too if I can. Is this the worst fate you can think of for me? It is no bad thing to be a chief, for it brings both riches and honour. Still, now that Ulysses is dead there are many great men in Ithaca both old and young, and some other may take the lead among them; nevertheless I will be chief in my own house, and will rule those whom Ulysses has won for me."

Then Eurymachus, son of Polybus, answered, "It rests with heaven to decide who shall be chief among us, but you shall be master in your own house and over your own

---

1　Danaans 指的是希腊人。

possessions; no one while there is a man in Ithaca shall do you violence nor rob you. And now, my good fellow, I want to know about this stranger. What country does he come from? Of what family is he, and where is his estate? Has he brought you news about the return of your father, or was he on business of his own? He seemed a well to do man, but he hurried off so suddenly that he was gone in a moment before we could get to know him."

"My father is dead and gone," answered Telemachus, "and even if some rumour reaches me I put no more faith in it now. My mother does indeed sometimes send for a soothsayer and question him, but I give his prophecyings no heed. As for the stranger, he was Mentes, son of Anchialus, chief of the Taphians, an old friend of my father's." But in his heart he knew that it had been the goddess.

...

(From Book I)

思考题

QUESTIONS

1 At the beginning of the book, the present condition of Ulysses is briefly stated, so is his future fate. Where is he now? What will await him if he arrives home?

2 There is a comparison between the fate of Ulysses and that of other heroes in which Agamemnon is particularly singled out. Why is Agamemnon mentioned? What is the role his story plays in the epic?

3 What is the advice Minerva gives Telemachus?

4 Why does Minerva mention Orestes, Agamemnon's son, when she gives advice to Telemachus?

5 From the conversation between Telemachus and Antinous, what can be known about the political regime of Ithaca, especially with reference to the position of the chief?

6 *The Odyssey* is mainly about the adventures of the hero Ulysses after the Trojan war, but in Book I his son Telemachus comes to the foreground instead of Ulysses. What do you expect to read in the following books? What are the other possible themes in addition to Ulysses' heroism?

7 Why do the suitors keep staying at Ulysses' home? What can you infer about the Greek custom of marriage?

8 When Telemachus bids his mother Penelope back to her place and asserts his mastership, Penelope can't help wondering (Page 10). What exactly does Penelope wonder at?

第二章

众人话旧 海伦还乡

导 读

　　本章选自《奥德赛》第四卷。此前的第二卷叙述了特勒马科斯在伊塔卡召集会议，宣布自己将要出海探寻父亲的消息。第三卷写了特勒马科斯访问尤利西斯在特洛伊战争中的战友涅斯托尔。在本章中特勒马科斯来到斯巴达，拜访了墨涅拉奥斯。墨涅拉奥斯和海伦讲述了尤利西斯在特洛伊战争中的英雄事迹，这些事迹没有在《伊利亚特》中得到叙述。墨涅拉奥斯还讲述了自己返乡的经历——他如何被困在埃及、如何受到老海神普罗透斯的指点，最终返回家园。当时普罗透斯还向他讲述了其他参加特洛伊战争的英雄的下落，告诉他尤利西斯仍然被卡吕普索稽留，阿伽门农回国后被埃吉斯托斯谋害，等等。

　　特洛伊战争的肇因海伦也在本章中现身，她在特洛伊陷落后随丈夫回到了斯巴达。古希腊在两性关系和婚姻方面的道德观念与中国的传统观念颇有不同之处，读者可以留心对比。特勒马科斯表明身份，说自己是尤利西斯之子，墨涅拉奥斯、海伦等一众人哭成一片，这一段描写极为动人。

They reached the low lying city of Lacedaemon, where they drove straight to the abode of Menelaus and found him in his own house, feasting with his many clansmen in honour of the wedding of his son, and also of his daughter, whom he was marrying to the son of that valiant warrior Achilles. He had given his consent and promised her to him while he was still at Troy, and now the gods were bringing the marriage about; so he was sending her with chariots and horses to the city of the Myrmidons over whom Achilles' son was reigning. For his only son he had found a bride from Sparta, the daughter of Alector. This son, Megapenthes, was born to him of a bondwoman, for heaven vouchsafed Helen no more children after she had borne Hermione, who was fair as golden Venus herself.

So the neighbours and kinsmen of Menelaus were feasting and making merry in his house. There was a bard also to sing to them and play his lyre, while two tumblers went about performing in the midst of them when the man struck up with his tune.

Telemachus and the son of Nestor[1] stayed their horses at the gate, whereon Eteoneus servant to Menelaus came out, and as soon as he saw them ran hurrying back into the house to tell his Master. He went close up to him and said, "Menelaus, there are some strangers come here, two men, who look like sons of Jove. What are we to do? Shall we take their

---

1 前文省略涅斯托尔派儿子护送特勒马科斯来斯巴达的内容。

horses out, or tell them to find friends elsewhere as they best can?"

Menelaus was very angry and said, "Eteoneus, son of Boethous, you never used to be a fool, but now you talk like a simpleton. Take their horses out, of course, and show the strangers in that they may have supper; you and I have staid often enough at other people's houses before we got back here, where heaven grant that we may rest in peace henceforward."

So Eteoneus bustled back and bade the other servants come with him. They took their sweating steeds from under the yoke, made them fast to the mangers, and gave them a feed of oats and barley mixed. Then they leaned the chariot against the end wall of the courtyard, and led the way into the house. Telemachus and Pisistratus[1] were astonished when they saw it, for its splendour was as that of the sun and moon; then, when they had admired everything to their heart's content, they went into the bath room and washed themselves.

When the servants had washed them and anointed them with oil, they brought them woollen cloaks and shirts, and the two took their seats by the side of Menelaus. A maidservant brought them water in a beautiful golden ewer, and poured it into a silver basin for them to wash their hands; and she drew a clean table beside them. An upper servant brought them bread, and offered them many good things of what there was in the house, while the carver fetched them plates of all manner of meats and set cups of gold by their side.

Menelaus then greeted them saying, "Fall to, and welcome; when you have done supper I shall ask who you are, for the lineage of such men as you cannot have been lost. You must be descended from a line of sceptre-bearing kings, for poor people do not have such sons as you are."

On this he handed them a piece of fat roast loin, which had been set near him as being a prime part, and they laid their hands on the good things that were before them; as soon as they had had enough to eat and drink, Telemachus said to the son of Nestor, with his head so close that no one might hear, "Look, Pisistratus, man after my own heart, see the gleam of bronze and gold—of amber, ivory, and silver. Everything is so splendid that it is like seeing the palace of Olympian Jove. I am lost in admiration."

Menelaus overheard him and said, "No one, my sons, can hold his own with Jove,

---

1 Pisistratus 是涅斯托尔的儿子。

for his house and everything about him is immortal; but among mortal men—well, there may be another who has as much wealth as I have, or there may not; but at all events I have travelled much and have undergone much hardship, for it was nearly eight years before I could get home with my fleet. I went to Cyprus, Phoenicia and the Egyptians; I went also to the Ethiopians, the Sidonians, and the Erembians, and to Libya where the lambs have horns as soon as they are born, and the sheep lamb down three times a year. Every one in that country, whether master or man, has plenty of cheese, meat, and good milk, for the ewes yield all the year round. But while I was travelling and getting great riches among these people, my brother was secretly and shockingly murdered through the perfidy of his wicked wife, so that I have no pleasure in being lord of all this wealth. Whoever your parents may be they must have told you about all this, and of my heavy loss in the ruin of a stately mansion fully and magnificently furnished. Would that I had only a third of what I now have so that I had stayed at home, and all those were living who perished on the plain of Troy, far from Argos. I often grieve, as I sit here in my house, for one and all of them. At times I cry aloud for sorrow, but presently I leave off again, for crying is cold comfort and one soon tires of it. Yet grieve for these as I may, I do so for one man more than for them all. I cannot even think of him without loathing both food and sleep, so miserable does he make me, for no one of all the Achaeans worked so hard or risked so much as he did. He took nothing by it, and has left a legacy of sorrow to myself, for he has been gone a long time, and we know not whether he is alive or dead. His old father, his long-suffering wife Penelope, and his son Telemachus, whom he left behind him an infant in arms, are plunged in grief on his account."

Thus spoke Menelaus, and the heart of Telemachus yearned as he bethought him of his father. Tears fell from his eyes as he heard him thus mentioned, so that he held his cloak before his face with both hands. When Menelaus saw this he doubted whether to let him choose his own time for speaking, or to ask him at once and find what it was all about.

While he was thus in two minds Helen came down from her high vaulted and perfumed room, looking as lovely as Diana herself. Adraste brought her a seat, Alcippe a soft woollen rug while Phylo fetched her the silver work-box which Alcandra wife of Polybus had given her. Polybus lived in Egyptian Thebes, which is the richest city in the whole world; he gave Menelaus two baths, both of pure silver, two tripods, and ten talents of gold; besides all this, his wife gave Helen some beautiful presents, to wit, a golden distaff, and a silver work box that ran on wheels, with a gold band round the top of it. Phylo now placed this by her side, full of fine spun yarn, and a distaff charged with violet coloured wool was laid upon the top of it. Then Helen took her seat, put her feet upon the footstool, and began to question her husband.

"Do we know, Menelaus," said she, "the names of these strangers who have come to visit us? Shall I guess right or wrong?—but I cannot help saying what I think. Never yet have I seen either man or woman so like somebody else (indeed when I look at him I hardly know what to think) as this young man is like Telemachus, whom Ulysses left as a baby behind him, when you Achaeans went to Troy with battle in your hearts, on account of my most shameless self."

"My dear wife," replied Menelaus, "I see the likeness just as you do. His hands and feet are just like Ulysses; so is his hair, with the shape of his head and the expression of his eyes. Moreover, when I was talking about Ulysses, and saying how much he had suffered on my account, tears fell from his eyes, and he hid his face in his mantle."

Then Pisistratus said, "Menelaus, son of Atreus, you are right in thinking that this young man is Telemachus, but he is very modest, and is ashamed to come here and begin opening up discourse with one whose conversation is so divinely interesting as your own. My father, Nestor, sent me to escort him hither, for he wanted to know whether you could give him any counsel or suggestion. A son has always trouble at home when his father has gone away leaving him without supporters; and this is how Telemachus is now placed, for his father is absent, and there is no one among his own people to stand by him."

"Bless my heart," replied Menelaus, "then I am receiving a visit from the son of a very dear friend, who suffered much hardship for my sake. I had always hoped to entertain him with most marked distinction when heaven had granted us a safe return from beyond the seas. I should have founded a city for him in Argos, and built him a house. I should have made him leave Ithaca with his goods, his son, and all his people, and should have sacked for them some one of the neighbouring cities that are subject to me. We should thus have seen one another continually, and nothing but death could have interrupted so close and happy an intercourse. I suppose, however, that heaven grudged us such great good fortune, for it has prevented the poor fellow from ever getting home at all."

Thus did he speak, and his words set them all a weeping. Helen wept, Telemachus wept, and so did Menelaus, nor could Pisistratus keep his eyes from filling, when he remembered his dear brother Antilochus whom the son of bright Dawn had killed. Thereon he said to Menelaus,

"Sir, my father Nestor, when we used to talk about you at home, told me you were a person of rare and excellent understanding. If, then, it be possible, do as I would urge you. I am not fond of crying while I am getting my supper. Morning will come in due course, and in the forenoon I care not how much I cry for those that are dead and gone. This is all we can do for the poor things. We can only shave our heads for them and wring the tears from our cheeks. I had a brother who died at Troy; he was by no means the worst man there; you are sure to have known him—his name was Antilochus; I never set eyes upon him myself, but they say that he was singularly fleet of foot and in fight valiant."

"Your discretion, my friend," answered Menelaus, "is beyond your years. It is plain you take after your father. One can soon see when a man is son to one whom heaven has blessed both as regards wife and offspring—and it has blessed Nestor from first to last all his days, giving him a green old age in his own house, with sons about him who are both well disposed and valiant. We will put an end therefore to all this weeping, and attend to our supper again. Let water be poured over our hands. Telemachus and I can talk with one another fully in the morning."

On this Asphalion, one of the servants, poured water over their hands and they laid their hands on the good things that were before them.

Then Jove's daughter Helen bethought her of another matter. She drugged the wine with an herb that banishes all care, sorrow, and ill humour. Whoever drinks wine thus drugged cannot shed a single tear all the rest of the day, not even though his father and mother both of them drop down dead, or he sees a brother or a son hewn in pieces before his very eyes. This drug, of such sovereign power and virtue, had been given to Helen by Polydamna wife of Thon, a woman of Egypt, where there grow all sorts of herbs, some good to put into the mixing bowl and others poisonous. Moreover, every one in the whole country is a skilled physician, for they are of the race of Paeeon. When Helen had put this drug in the bowl, and had told the servants to serve the wine round, she said:

"Menelaus, son of Atreus, and you my good friends, sons of honourable men (which is as Jove wills, for he is the giver both of good and evil, and can do what he chooses), feast here as you will, and listen while I tell you a tale in season. I cannot indeed name every single one of the exploits of Ulysses, but I can say what he did when he was before Troy, and you Achaeans were in all sorts of difficulties. He covered himself with wounds and bruises, dressed himself all in rags, and entered the enemy's city looking like a menial or a beggar, and quite different from what he did when he was among his own people. In this disguise he entered the city of Troy, and no one said anything to him. I alone recognised him and began to question him, but he was too cunning for me. When, however, I had washed and anointed him and had given him clothes, and after I had sworn a solemn oath not to betray him to the Trojans till he had got safely back to his own camp and to the ships, he told me all that the Achaeans meant to do. He killed many Trojans and got much information before he reached the Argive camp, for all which things the Trojan women made lamentation, but for my own part I was glad, for my heart was beginning to yearn after my home, and I was unhappy about the wrong that Venus had done me in taking me over there, away from my country, my girl, and my lawful wedded husband, who is indeed by no means deficient either in person or understanding."

Then Menelaus said, "All that you have been saying, my dear wife, is true. I have travelled much, and have had much to do with heroes, but I have never seen such another man as Ulysses. What endurance too, and what courage he displayed within the wooden horse, wherein all the bravest of the Argives were lying in wait to bring death and destruction upon the Trojans. At that moment you came up to us; some god who wished well to the Trojans must have set you on to it and you had Deiphobus with you. Three times did you go all round our hiding place and pat it; you called our chiefs each by his own name, and mimicked all our wives—Diomed, Ulysses, and I from our seats inside heard what a noise you made. Diomed and I could not make up our minds whether to spring out then and there, or to answer you from inside, but Ulysses held us all in check, so we sat quite still, all except Anticlus, who was beginning to answer you, when Ulysses clapped his two brawny hands over his mouth, and kept them there. It was this that saved us all, for he muzzled Anticlus till Minerva took you away again."

"How sad," exclaimed Telemachus, "that all this was of no avail to save him, nor yet his own iron courage. But now, sir, be pleased to send us all to bed, that we may lie down and enjoy the blessed boon of sleep."

On this Helen told the maid servants to set beds in the room that was in the gatehouse, and to make them with good red rugs, and spread coverlets on the top of them with woollen cloaks for the guests to wear. So the maids went out, carrying a torch, and made the beds, to which a man-servant presently conducted the strangers. Thus, then, did Telemachus and Pisistratus sleep there in the forecourt, while the son of Atreus lay in an inner room with lovely Helen by his side.

When the child of morning, rosy-fingered Dawn appeared, Menelaus rose and dressed himself. He bound his sandals on to his comely feet, girded his sword about his shoulders, and left his room looking like an immortal god. Then, taking a seat near Telemachus he said:

"And what, Telemachus, has led you to take this long sea voyage to Lacedaemon[1]? Are you on public, or private business? Tell me all about it."

"I have come, sir," replied Telemachus, "to see if you can tell me anything about my father. I am being eaten out of house and home; my fair estate is being wasted, and my house is full of miscreants who keep killing great numbers of my sheep and oxen, on the pretence of paying their addresses to my mother. Therefore, I am suppliant at your knees if haply you may tell me about my father's melancholy end, whether you saw it with your own eyes, or heard it from some other traveller; for he was a man born to trouble. Do not soften things out of any pity for myself, but tell me in all plainness exactly what you saw. If my brave father Ulysses ever did you loyal service either by word or deed, when you Achaeans were harassed by the Trojans, bear it in mind now as in my favour and tell me truly all."

Menelaus on hearing this was very much shocked. "So," he exclaimed, "these cowards would usurp a brave man's bed? A hind might as well lay her new born young in the lair of a lion, and then go off to feed in the forest or in some grassy dell: the lion when he comes back to his lair will make short work with the pair of them—and so will Ulysses with these suitors. By father Jove, Minerva, and Apollo, if Ulysses is still the man that he was when he wrestled with Philomeleides in Lesbos, and threw him so heavily that all the Achaeans cheered him—if he is still such and were to come near these suitors, they would have a short shrift and a sorry wedding. As regards your questions, however, I will not prevaricate nor deceive you, but will tell you without concealment all that the old man of the sea[2] told me.

1　Lacedaemon 是古斯巴达的别称。

2　这指的是海里的一位神祇，名叫 Proteus。

"I was trying to come on here, but the gods detained me in Egypt, for my hecatombs had not given them full satisfaction, and the gods are very strict about having their dues. Now off Egypt, about as far as a ship can sail in a day with a good stiff breeze behind her, there is an island called Pharos—it has a good harbour from which vessels can get out into open sea when they have taken in water—and here the gods becalmed me twenty days without so much as a breath of fair wind to help me forward. We should have run clean out of provisions and my men would have starved, if a goddess had not taken pity upon me and saved me in the person of Idothea, daughter to Proteus, the old man of the sea, for she had taken a great fancy to me.

"She came to me one day when I was by myself, as I often was, for the men used to go with their barbed hooks, all over the island in the hope of catching a fish or two to save them from the pangs of hunger. 'Stranger,' said she, 'it seems to me that you like starving in this way—at any rate it does not greatly trouble you, for you stick here day after day, without even trying to get away though your men are dying by inches.'

"'Let me tell you,' said I, 'whichever of the goddesses you may happen to be, that I am not staying here of my own accord, but must have offended the gods that live in heaven. Tell me, therefore, for the gods know everything, which of the immortals it is that is hindering me in this way, and tell me also how I may sail the sea so as to reach my home.'

"'Stranger,' replied she, 'I will make it all quite clear to you. There is an old immortal who lives under the sea hereabouts and whose name is Proteus. He is an Egyptian, and people say he is my father; he is Neptune's head man and knows every inch of ground all over the bottom of the sea. If you can snare him and hold him tight, he will tell you about your voyage, what courses you are to take, and how you are to sail the sea so as to reach your home. He will also tell you, if you so will, all that has been going on at your house both good and bad, while you have been away on your long and dangerous journey.'

"'Can you show me,' said I, 'some stratagem by means of which I may catch this old god without his suspecting it and finding me out? For a god is not easily caught—not by a mortal man.'

"'Stranger,' said she, 'I will make it all quite clear to you. About the time when the sun shall have reached mid heaven, the old man of the sea comes up from under the waves, heralded by the West wind that furs the water over his head. As soon as he has come up he lies down, and goes to sleep in a great sea cave, where the seals—Halosydne's[1] chickens as they call them—come up also from the grey sea, and go to sleep in shoals all round him; and a very strong and fish-like smell do they bring with them. Early to-morrow morning I will take you to this place and will lay you in ambush. Pick out, therefore, the three best men you have in your fleet, and I will tell you all the tricks that the old man will play you.

"'First he will look over all his seals, and count them; then, when he has seen them and tallied them on his five fingers, he will go to sleep among them, as a shepherd among his sheep. The moment you see that he is asleep seize him; put forth all your strength and hold him fast, for he will do his very utmost to get away from you. He will turn himself into every kind of creature that goes upon the earth, and will become also both fire and water; but you must hold him fast and grip him tighter and tighter, till he begins to talk to you and comes back to what he was when you saw him go to sleep; then you may slacken your hold and let him go; and you can ask him which of the gods it is that is angry with you, and what you must do to reach your home over the seas.'

"Having so said she dived under the waves, whereon I turned back to the place where my ships were ranged upon the shore; and my heart was clouded with care as I went along. When I reached my ship we got supper ready, for night was falling, and camped down upon the beach.

"When the child of morning, rosy-fingered Dawn appeared, I took the three men on whose prowess of all kinds I could most rely, and went along by the sea-side, praying heartily to heaven. Meanwhile the goddess fetched me up four seal skins from the bottom of the sea, all of them just skinned, for she meant playing a trick upon her father. Then she dug four pits for us to lie in, and sat down to wait till we should come up. When we were close to her, she made us lie down in the pits one after the other, and threw a seal skin over each of us. Our ambuscade would have been intolerable, for the stench of the fishy seals was most distressing—who would go to bed with a sea monster if he could help it?—but here, too, the goddess helped us, and thought of something that gave us great relief, for she put some ambrosia under each man's nostrils, which was so fragrant that it killed the smell of the seals.

"We waited the whole morning and made the best of it, watching the seals come up in

---

1　Halosydne 是海王后安菲特里忒（Amphitrite）的姓氏。

hundreds to bask upon the sea shore, till at noon the old man of the sea came up too, and when he had found his fat seals he went over them and counted them. We were among the first he counted, and he never suspected any guile, but laid himself down to sleep as soon as he had done counting. Then we rushed upon him with a shout and seized him; on which he began at once with his old tricks, and changed himself first into a lion with a great mane; then all of a sudden he became a dragon, a leopard, a wild boar; the next moment he was running water, and then again directly he was a tree, but we stuck to him and never lost hold, till at last the cunning old creature became distressed, and said, 'Which of the gods was it, Son of Atreus, that hatched this plot with you for snaring me and seizing me against my will? What do you want?'

"'You know that yourself, old man,' I answered, 'you will gain nothing by trying to put me off. It is because I have been kept so long in this island, and see no sign of my being able to get away. I am losing all heart; tell me, then, for you gods know everything, which of the immortals it is that is hindering me, and tell me also how I may sail the sea so as to reach my home?'

"'Then,' he said, 'if you would finish your voyage and get home quickly, you must offer sacrifices to Jove and to the rest of the gods before embarking; for it is decreed that you shall not get back to your friends, and to your own house, till you have returned to the heaven-fed stream of Egypt, and offered holy hecatombs to the immortal gods that reign in heaven. When you have done this they will let you finish your voyage.'

"I was broken hearted when I heard that I must go back all that long and terrible voyage to Egypt; nevertheless, I answered, 'I will do all, old man, that you have laid upon me; but now tell me, and tell me true, whether all the Achaeans whom Nestor and I left behind us when we set sail from Troy have got home safely, or whether any one of them came to a bad end either on board his own ship or among his friends when the days of his fighting were done.'

"'Son of Atreus,' he answered, 'why ask me? You had better not know what I can tell you, for your eyes will surely fill when you have heard my story. Many of those about whom you ask are dead and gone, but many still remain, and only two of the chief men among the Achaeans perished during their return home. As for what happened on the field of battle—you were there yourself. A third Achaean leader is still at sea, alive, but hindered from returning. Ajax[1] was wrecked, for Neptune drove him on to the great rocks of Gyrae; nevertheless, he let him get safe out of the water, and in spite of all Minerva's hatred he would have escaped death, if he had not ruined himself by boasting. He said the gods could not drown him even though they had tried to do so, and when Neptune heard this large talk, he seized his trident in his two brawny hands, and split the rock of Gyrae in two pieces. The base remained where it was, but the part on which Ajax was sitting fell headlong into the sea and carried Ajax with it; so he drank salt water and was drowned.

"'Your brother and his ships escaped, for Juno protected him, but when he was just about to reach the high promontory of Malea, he was caught by a heavy gale which carried him out to sea again sorely against his will, and drove him to the foreland where Thyestes used to dwell, but where Aegisthus was then living. By and by, however, it seemed as though he was to return safely after all, for the gods backed the wind into its old quarter and they reached home; whereon Agamemnon kissed his native soil, and shed tears of joy at finding himself in his own country.

"'Now there was a watchman whom Aegisthus kept always on the watch, and to whom he had promised two talents of gold. This man had been looking out for a whole year to make sure that Agamemnon did not give him the slip and prepare war; when, therefore, this man saw Agamemnon go by, he went and told Aegisthus, who at once began to lay a plot for him. He picked twenty of his bravest warriors and placed them in ambuscade on one side the cloister, while on the opposite side he prepared a banquet. Then he sent his chariots and horsemen to Agamemnon, and invited him to the feast, but he meant foul play. He got him there, all unsuspicious of the doom that was awaiting him, and killed him when the banquet was over as though he were butchering an ox in the shambles; not one of Agamemnon's followers was left alive, nor yet one of Aegisthus', but they were all killed there in the cloisters.'

"Thus spoke Proteus, and I was broken hearted as I heard him. I sat down upon the sands and wept; I felt as though I could no longer bear to live nor look upon the light of the sun. Presently, when I had had my fill of weeping and writhing upon the ground, the old man of the sea said, 'Son of Atreus, do not waste any more time in crying so bitterly; it can do no manner of good; find your way home as fast as ever you can, for Aegisthus may be

---

1　Ajax 指的是小埃阿斯，不是死在特洛伊的大埃阿斯，后者会在后文出现。

still alive, and even though Orestes has been beforehand with you in killing him, you may yet come in for his funeral.'

"On this I took comfort in spite of all my sorrow, and said, 'I know, then, about these two; tell me, therefore, about the third man of whom you spoke; is he still alive, but at sea, and unable to get home? or is he dead? Tell me, no matter how much it may grieve me.'

"'The third man,' he answered, 'is Ulysses who dwells in Ithaca. I can see him in an island sorrowing bitterly in the house of the nymph Calypso, who is keeping him prisoner, and he cannot reach his home for he has no ships nor sailors to take him over the sea. As for your own end, Menelaus, you shall not die in Argos, but the gods will take you to the Elysian plain, which is at the ends of the world. There fair-haired Rhadamanthus reigns, and men lead an easier life than any where else in the world, for in Elysium there falls not rain, nor hail, nor snow, but Oceanus breathes ever with a West wind that sings softly from the sea, and gives fresh life to all men. This will happen to you because you have married Helen, and are Jove's son-in-law.'

"As he spoke he dived under the waves, whereon I turned back to the ships with my companions, and my heart was clouded with care as I went along. When we reached the ships we got supper ready, for night was falling, and camped down upon the beach. When the child of morning, rosy-fingered Dawn appeared, we drew our ships into the water, and put our masts and sails within them; then we went on board ourselves, took our seats on the benches, and smote the grey sea with our oars. I again stationed my ships in the heaven-fed stream of Egypt, and offered hecatombs that were full and sufficient. When I had thus appeased heaven's anger, I raised a barrow to the memory of Agamemnon that his name might live for ever, after which I had a quick passage home, for the gods sent me a fair wind."

...[1]

(From Book IV)

---

1 墨涅拉奥斯讲完后，众人准备宴席，同时在伊塔卡，求婚人计划谋害特勒马科斯。

思考题

QUESTIONS

1 Nestor's son Pisistatrus accompanies Telemachus to Sparta. What can you infer about the host-guest relationship in Greece?

2 When Helen appears, she is doing spinning. What is the color of the wool she is spinning? Keep it in mind and find out places in other chapters where the color of wool or clothes is mentioned.

3 Menelaus and Helen relate stories of Ulysses in the Trojan war, which is not told in *The Iliad*. What is the image of Ulysses like in the memory of his old comrade and his wife?

4 What is the imagination of Egypt by the Greeks? In what ways are the Egyptians different from Greeks?

5 What is the fate of Helen after the sack of Troy? Does she regret for eloping with Paris?

6 How many times does the phrase "the child of morning, rosy-fingered Dawn" appear in the excerpt? How do you understand the repetition? Try to notice other repetitions in your reading.

7 Ajax died of a sin condemned by the Greeks. What is that?

8 Describe the way Telemachus is received by Menelaus.

第三章

女神割爱
英雄出海

导读

INTRODUCTION

本章选自《奥德赛》第五卷。墨丘利受朱庇特派遣，来到女神卡吕普索居住的奥古吉埃岛，令其释放尤利西斯，女神虽心有不甘，但不得不遵从众神之王的命令。尤利西斯遂伐木造船，出海归国，不料途中又遇风暴，历经艰险后终于在斯克里埃岛上岸。

尤利西斯被卡吕普索所困时，曾独坐海边，望洋兴叹。这是一段画面感很强的生动描写，值得认真体会。本卷中还有多处精彩的细节描写，例如借墨丘利的视角对卡吕普索居处的观察，通过描写尤利西斯如何建造海船来表现他的智巧。此外，卡吕普索不愿放走尤利西斯时，对墨丘利的回话，可以从女性主义的角度进行解读。这些段落文笔精妙，含义丰富，阅读时值得仔细咀嚼体会。

选文

SELECTION

And now, as Dawn rose from her couch beside Tithonus—harbinger of light alike to mortals and immortals—the gods met in council and with them, Jove the lord of thunder, who is their king. Thereon Minerva began to tell them of the many sufferings of Ulysses, for she pitied him away there in the house of the nymph Calypso.

"Father Jove," said she, "and all you other gods that live in everlasting bliss, I hope there may never be such a thing as a kind and well-disposed ruler any more, nor one who will govern equitably. I hope they will be all henceforth cruel and unjust, for there is not one of his subjects but has forgotten Ulysses, who ruled them as though he were their father. There he is, lying in great pain in an island where dwells the nymph Calypso, who will not let him go; and he cannot get back to his own country, for he can find neither ships nor sailors to take him over the sea. Furthermore, wicked people are now trying to murder his only son Telemachus, who is coming home from Pylos and Lacedaemon, where he has been to see if he can get news of his father."

"What, my dear, are you talking about?" replied her father, "did you not send him there yourself, because you thought it would help Ulysses to get home and punish the suitors? Besides, you are perfectly able to protect Telemachus, and to see him safely home again, while the suitors have to come hurry-skurrying back without having killed him."

When he had thus spoken, he said to his son Mercury, "Mercury, you are our messenger, go therefore and tell Calypso we have decreed that poor Ulysses is to return home. He is to be convoyed neither by gods nor men, but after a perilous voyage of twenty days upon a raft he is to reach fertile Scheria, the land of the Phaeacians, who are near of kin to the gods, and will honour him as though he were one of ourselves. They will send him in a ship to his own country, and will give him more bronze and gold and raiment than he would have brought back from Troy, if he had had all his prize money and had got home without disaster. This is how we have settled that he shall return to his country and his friends."

...[1]

He found her[2] at home. There was a large fire burning on the hearth, and one could smell from far the fragrant reek of burning cedar and sandal wood. As for herself, she was busy at her loom, shooting her golden shuttle through the warp and singing beautifully. Round her cave there was a thick wood of alder, poplar, and sweet smelling cypress trees, wherein all kinds of great birds had built their nests—owls, hawks, and chattering sea-crows that occupy their business in the waters. A vine loaded with grapes was trained and grew luxuriantly about the mouth of the cave; there were also four running rills of water in channels cut pretty close together, and turned hither and thither so as to irrigate the beds of violets and luscious herbage over which they flowed. Even a god could not help being charmed with such a lovely spot, so Mercury stood still and looked at it; but when he had admired it sufficiently he went inside the cave.

Calypso knew him at once—for the gods all know each other, no matter how far they live from one another—but Ulysses was not within; he was on the sea-shore as usual, looking out upon the barren ocean with tears in his eyes, groaning and breaking his heart for sorrow. Calypso gave Mercury a seat and said: "Why have you come to see me, Mercury—honoured, and ever welcome—for you do not visit me often? Say what you want; I will do it for you at once if I can, and if it can be done at all; but come inside, and let me set refreshment before you."

As she spoke she drew a table loaded with ambrosia beside him and mixed him some red nectar, so Mercury ate and drank till he had had enough, and then said:

---

1 此处省略墨丘利（Mercury）下界来到卡吕普索（Calypso）的岛屿。

2 her 指的是卡吕普索；He 指的是墨丘利。

"We are speaking god and goddess to one another, and you ask me why I have come here, and I will tell you truly as you would have me do. Jove sent me; it was no doing of mine; who could possibly want to come all this way over the sea where there are no cities full of people to offer me sacrifices or choice hecatombs? Nevertheless I had to come, for none of us other gods can cross Jove, nor transgress his orders. He says that you have here the most ill-starred of all those who fought nine years before the city of King Priam[1] and sailed home in the tenth year after having sacked it. On their way home they sinned against Minerva, who raised both wind and waves against them, so that all his brave companions perished, and he alone was carried hither by wind and tide. Jove says that you are to let this man go at once, for it is decreed that he shall not perish here, far from his own people, but shall return to his house and country and see his friends again."

Calypso trembled with rage when she heard this, "You gods," she exclaimed, "ought to be ashamed of yourselves. You are always jealous and hate seeing a goddess take a fancy to a mortal man, and live with him in open matrimony. So when rosy-fingered Dawn made love to Orion, you precious gods were all of you furious till Diana went and killed him in Ortygia. So again when Ceres fell in love with Iasion, and yielded to him in a thrice-ploughed fallow field, Jove came to hear of it before so very long and killed Iasion with his thunderbolts. And now you are angry with me too because I have a man here. I found the poor creature sitting all alone astride of a keel, for Jove had struck his ship with lightning and sunk it in mid ocean, so that all his crew were drowned, while he himself was driven by wind and waves on to my island. I got fond of him and cherished him, and had set my heart on making him immortal, so that he should never grow old all his days; still I cannot cross Jove, nor bring his counsels to nothing; therefore, if he insists upon it, let the man go beyond the seas again; but I cannot send him anywhere myself for I have neither ships nor men who can take him. Nevertheless I will readily give him such advice, in all good faith, as will be likely to bring him safely to his own country."

"Then send him away," said Mercury, "or Jove will be angry with you and punish you."

On this he took his leave, and Calypso went out to look for Ulysses, for she had heard Jove's message. She found him sitting upon the beach with his eyes ever filled with tears, and dying of sheer home sickness; for he had got tired of Calypso, and though he was forced

---

1　Priam 是特洛伊的国王。

to sleep with her in the cave by night, it was she, not he, that would have it so. As for the day time, he spent it on the rocks and on the sea shore, weeping, crying aloud for his despair, and always looking out upon the sea. Calypso then went close up to him said:

"My poor fellow, you shall not stay here grieving and fretting your life out any longer. I am going to send you away of my own free will; so go, cut some beams of wood, and make yourself a large raft with an upper deck that it may carry you safely over the sea. I will put bread, wine, and water on board to save you from starving. I will also give you clothes, and will send you a fair wind to take you home, if the gods in heaven so will it—for they know more about these things, and can settle them better than I can."

Ulysses shuddered as he heard her. "Now goddess," he answered, "there is something behind all this; you cannot be really meaning to help me home when you bid me do such a dreadful thing as put to sea on a raft. Not even a well found ship with a fair wind could venture on such a distant voyage: nothing that you can say or do shall make me go on board a raft unless you first solemnly swear that you mean me no mischief."

Calypso smiled at this and caressed him with her hand: "You know a great deal," said she, "but you are quite wrong here. May heaven above and earth below be my witnesses, with the waters of the river Styx[1]—and this is the most solemn oath which a blessed god can take—that I mean you no sort of harm, and am only advising you to do exactly what I should do myself in your place. I am dealing with you quite straightforwardly; my heart is not made of iron, and I am very sorry for you."

When she had thus spoken she led the way rapidly before him, and Ulysses followed in her steps; so the pair, goddess and man, went on and on till they came to Calypso's cave, where Ulysses took the seat that Mercury had just left. Calypso set meat and drink before him of the food that mortals eat; but her maids brought ambrosia and nectar for herself, and they laid their hands on the good things that were before them. When they had satisfied themselves with meat and drink, Calypso spoke, saying:

"Ulysses, noble son of Laertes, so you would start home to your own land at once? Good luck go with you, but if you could only know how much suffering is in store for you before you get back to your own country, you would stay where you are, keep house along

---

1 Styx 是冥界的一条河，无论是凡人还是神明，对着这条河发出的誓愿均不可违背。

with me, and let me make you immortal, no matter how anxious you may be to see this wife of yours, of whom you are thinking all the time day after day; yet I flatter myself that I am no whit less tall or well-looking than she is, for it is not to be expected that a mortal woman should compare in beauty with an immortal."

"Goddess," replied Ulysses, "do not be angry with me about this. I am quite aware that my wife Penelope is nothing like so tall or so beautiful as yourself. She is only a woman, whereas you are an immortal. Nevertheless, I want to get home, and can think of nothing else. If some god wrecks me when I am on the sea, I will bear it and make the best of it. I have had infinite trouble both by land and sea already, so let this go with the rest."

Presently the sun set and it became dark, whereon the pair retired into the inner part of the cave and went to bed.

When the child of morning rosy-fingered Dawn appeared, Ulysses put on his shirt and cloak, while the goddess wore a dress of a light gossamer fabric, very fine and graceful, with a beautiful golden girdle about her waist and a veil to cover her head. She at once set herself to think how she could speed Ulysses on his way. So she gave him a great bronze axe that suited his hands; it was sharpened on both sides, and had a beautiful olive-wood handle fitted firmly on to it. She also gave him a sharp adze, and then led the way to the far end of the island where the largest trees grew—alder, poplar and pine, that reached the sky—very dry and well seasoned, so as to sail light for him in the water. Then, when she had shown him where the best trees grew, Calypso went home, leaving him to cut them, which he soon finished doing. He cut down twenty trees in all and adzed them smooth, squaring them by rule in good workmanlike fashion. Meanwhile Calypso came back with some augers, so he bored holes with them and fitted the timbers together with bolts and rivets. He made the raft as broad as a skilled shipwright makes the beam of a large vessel, and he fixed a deck on top of the ribs, and ran a gunwale all round it. He also made a mast with a yard arm, and a rudder to steer with. He fenced the raft all round with wicker hurdles as a protection against the waves, and then he threw on a quantity of wood. By and by Calypso brought him some linen to make the sails, and he made these too, excellently, making them fast with braces and sheets. Last of all, with the help of levers, he drew the raft down into the water.

In four days he had completed the whole work, and on the fifth Calypso sent him from the island after washing him and giving him some clean clothes. She gave him a goat skin full of black wine, and another larger one of water; she also gave him a wallet full of provisions, and found him in much good meat. Moreover, she made the wind fair and warm for him, and gladly did Ulysses spread his sail before it, while he sat and guided the raft skilfully by means of the rudder. He never closed his eyes, but kept them fixed on the Pleiads, on late-setting Bootes, and on the Bear—which men also call the Wain, and which turns round and round where it is, facing Orion, and alone never dipping into the stream of Oceanus—for Calypso had told him to keep this to his left. Days seven and ten did he sail over the sea, and on the eighteenth the dim outlines of the mountains on the nearest part of the Phaeacian coast appeared, rising like a shield on the horizon.

But King Neptune, who was returning from the Ethiopians, caught sight of Ulysses a long way off, from the mountains of the Solymi. He could see him sailing upon the sea, and it made him very angry, so he wagged his head and muttered to himself, saying, "Good heavens, so the gods have been changing their minds about Ulysses while I was away in Ethiopia, and now he is close to the land of the Phaeacians, where it is decreed that he shall escape from the calamities that have befallen him. Still, he shall have plenty of hardship yet before he has done with it."

Thereon he gathered his clouds together, grasped his trident, stirred it round in the sea, and roused the rage of every wind that blows till earth, sea, and sky were hidden in cloud, and night sprang forth out of the heavens. Winds from East, South, North, and West fell upon him all at the same time, and a tremendous sea got up, so that Ulysses' heart began to fail him. "Alas," he said to himself in his dismay, "what ever will become of me? I am afraid Calypso was right when she said I should have trouble by sea before I got back home. It is all coming true. How black is Jove making heaven with his clouds, and what a sea the winds are raising from every quarter at once. I am now safe to perish. Blest and thrice blest were those Danaans who fell before Troy in the cause of the sons of Atreus[1]. Would that I had been killed on the day when the Trojans were pressing me so sorely about the dead body of Achilles, for then I should have had due burial and the Achaeans would have honoured my name; but now it seems that I shall come to a most pitiable end."

As he spoke a sea broke over him with such terrific fury that the raft reeled again, and he was carried overboard a long way off. He let go the helm, and the force of the hurricane was so great that it broke the mast half way up, and both sail and yard went over into the

---

1 Atreus 是阿伽门农和墨涅拉奥斯的父亲，他们兄弟二人召集希腊联军对特洛伊发动了战争。

sea. For a long time Ulysses was under water, and it was all he could do to rise to the surface again, for the clothes Calypso had given him weighed him down; but at last he got his head above water and spat out the bitter brine that was running down his face in streams. In spite of all this, however, he did not lose sight of his raft, but swam as fast as he could towards it, got hold of it, and climbed on board again so as to escape drowning. The sea took the raft and tossed it about as Autumn winds whirl thistledown round and round upon a road. It was as though the South, North, East, and West winds were all playing battledore and shuttlecock with it at once.

When he was in this plight, Ino daughter of Cadmus, also called Leucothea, saw him. She had formerly been a mere mortal, but had been since raised to the rank of a marine goddess. Seeing in what great distress Ulysses now was, she had compassion upon him, and, rising like a sea-gull from the waves, took her seat upon the raft.

"My poor good man," said she, "why is Neptune so furiously angry with you? He is giving you a great deal of trouble, but for all his bluster he will not kill you. You seem to be a sensible person, do then as I bid you; strip, leave your raft to drive before the wind, and swim to the Phaeacian coast where better luck awaits you. And here, take my veil and put it round your chest; it is enchanted, and you can come to no harm so long as you wear it. As soon as you touch land take it off, throw it back as far as you can into the sea, and then go away again." With these words she took off her veil and gave it him. Then she dived down again like a sea-gull and vanished beneath the dark blue waters.

But Ulysses did not know what to think. "Alas," he said to himself in his dismay, "this is only some one or other of the gods who is luring me to ruin by advising me to quit my raft. At any rate I will not do so at present, for the land where she said I should be quit of all troubles seemed to be still a good way off. I know what I will do—I am sure it will be best— no matter what happens I will stick to the raft as long as her timbers hold together, but when the sea breaks her up I will swim for it; I do not see how I can do any better than this."

While he was thus in two minds, Neptune sent a terrible great wave that seemed to rear itself above his head till it broke right over the raft, which then went to pieces as though it were a heap of dry chaff tossed about by a whirlwind. Ulysses got astride of one plank and rode upon it as if he were on horseback; he then took off the clothes Calypso had given him, bound Ino's veil under his arms, and plunged into the sea—meaning to swim on shore. King Neptune watched him as he did so, and wagged his head, muttering to himself and saying,

"There now, swim up and down as you best can till you fall in with well-to-do people. I do not think you will be able to say that I have let you off too lightly." On this he lashed his horses and drove to Aegae where his palace is.

But Minerva resolved to help Ulysses, so she bound the ways of all the winds except one, and made them lie quite still; but she roused a good stiff breeze from the North that should lay the waters till Ulysses reached the land of the Phaeacians where he would be safe.

Thereon he floated about for two nights and two days in the water, with a heavy swell on the sea and death staring him in the face; but when the third day broke, the wind fell and there was a dead calm without so much as a breath of air stirring. As he rose on the swell he looked eagerly ahead, and could see land quite near. Then, as children rejoice when their dear father begins to get better after having for a long time borne sore affliction sent him by some angry spirit, but the gods deliver him from evil, so was Ulysses thankful when he again saw land and trees, and swam on with all his strength that he might once more set foot upon dry ground. When, however, he got within earshot, he began to hear the surf thundering up against the rocks, for the swell still broke against them with a terrific roar. Everything was enveloped in spray; there were no harbours where a ship might ride, nor shelter of any kind, but only headlands, low-lying rocks, and mountain tops.

Ulysses' heart now began to fail him, and he said despairingly to himself, "Alas, Jove has let me see land after swimming so far that I had given up all hope, but I can find no landing place, for the coast is rocky and surf-beaten, the rocks are smooth and rise sheer from the sea, with deep water close under them so that I cannot climb out for want of foot hold. I am afraid some great wave will lift me off my legs and dash me against the rocks as I leave the water—which would give me a sorry landing. If, on the other hand, I swim further in search of some shelving beach or harbour, a hurricane may carry me out to sea again sorely against my will, or heaven may send some great monster of the deep to attack me; for Amphitrite[1] breeds many such, and I know that Neptune is very angry with me."

While he was thus in two minds a wave caught him and took him with such force against the rocks that he would have been smashed and torn to pieces if Minerva had not shown him what to do. He caught hold of the rock with both hands and clung to it groaning with pain till the wave retired, so he was saved that time; but presently the wave came on

---

1 Amphitrite 是海王 Neptune 的妻子。

again and carried him back with it far into the sea—tearing his hands as the suckers of a polypus are torn when some one plucks it from its bed, and the stones come up along with it—even so did the rocks tear the skin from his strong hands, and then the wave drew him deep down under the water.

Here poor Ulysses would have certainly perished even in spite of his own destiny, if Minerva had not helped him to keep his wits about him. He swam seaward again, beyond reach of the surf that was beating against the land, and at the same time he kept looking towards the shore to see if he could find some haven, or a spit that should take the waves aslant. By and by, as he swam on, he came to the mouth of a river, and here he thought would be the best place, for there were no rocks, and it afforded shelter from the wind. He felt that there was a current, so he prayed inwardly and said:

"Hear me, O King, whoever you may be, and save me from the anger of the sea-god Neptune, for I approach you prayerfully. Any one who has lost his way has at all times a claim even upon the gods, wherefore in my distress I draw near to your stream, and cling to the knees of your riverhood. Have mercy upon me, O king, for I declare myself your suppliant."

Then the god staid his stream and stilled the waves, making all calm before him, and bringing him safely into the mouth of the river. Here at last Ulysses' knees and strong hands failed him, for the sea had completely broken him. His body was all swollen, and his mouth and nostrils ran down like a river with sea-water, so that he could neither breathe nor speak, and lay swooning from sheer exhaustion; presently, when he had got his breath and came to himself again, he took off the scarf that Ino had given him and threw it back into the salt stream of the river, whereon Ino received it into her hands from the wave that bore it towards her. Then he left the river, laid himself down among the rushes, and kissed the bounteous earth.

"Alas," he cried to himself in his dismay, "what ever will become of me, and how is it all to end? If I stay here upon the river bed through the long watches of the night, I am so exhausted that the bitter cold and damp may make an end of me—for towards sunrise there will be a keen wind blowing from off the river. If, on the other hand, I climb the hill side, find shelter in the woods, and sleep in some thicket, I may escape the cold and have a good night's rest, but some savage beast may take advantage of me and devour me."

In the end he deemed it best to take to the woods, and he found one upon some high ground not far from the water. There he crept beneath two shoots of olive that grew from a single stock—the one an ungrafted sucker, while the other had been grafted. No wind, however squally, could break through the cover they afforded, nor could the sun's rays pierce them, nor the rain get through them, so closely did they grow into one another. Ulysses crept under these and began to make himself a bed to lie on, for there was a great litter of dead leaves lying about—enough to make a covering for two or three men even in hard winter weather. He was glad enough to see this, so he laid himself down and heaped the leaves all round him. Then, as one who lives alone in the country, far from any neighbor, hides a brand as fire-seed in the ashes to save himself from having to get a light elsewhere, even so did Ulysses cover himself up with leaves; and Minerva shed a sweet sleep upon his eyes, closed his eyelids, and made him lose all memories of his sorrows.

(From Book V)

思考题

QUESTIONS

1 At the beginning of the book the Olympians are having a council in which the fate of Ulysses is discussed. What value does Minerva appeal to when she speaks for Ulysses? What qualities is a ruler supposed to have?

2 Calypso is fond of Ulysses and wants to make him immortal. Why then does Ulysses still want to go back home?

3 What do the immortals have for food? What do the mortals eat?

4 Greek gods often have their favorite places on earth. Neptune stays at his favorite place when the Olympians are having a council. What is his favorite place?

5 Which way of death does Ulysses prefer, death on the battlefield or on the sea? What values does it reflect?

6 Ulysses is often said to be "in two minds". Give examples from the book.

7 Many metaphors are used in the book. Find them out and see what they have in common.

8 Ulysses is a good orator. Pay attention to his talk with Calypso and see how he manifests his eloquence.

第四章

劫后余生
巧遇公主

导读

INTRODUCTION

　　本章选自《奥德赛》第六卷，故事紧接上一章，讲述了尤利西斯告别女神卡吕普索，从奥古吉埃岛启程回家，中途遇上风暴，停靠在费埃克斯人居住的斯克里埃岛的故事。正巧遇到费埃克斯人的公主瑙西卡和侍女们在水边浣衣，于是尤利西斯向公主求助。公主见他言辞巧妙，举止有礼，便令他沐浴更衣，供他饱食足饮，然后驾车引导他进入城市。

　　这一章的内容是尤利西斯整个历险的转折点。奥古吉埃岛是他回到故国伊塔卡之前的最后一站。当地人的风俗与他此前在历险中遇到的各地风俗都不一样，却与尤利西斯本国的风俗更为接近。尤利西斯进入国王阿尔基诺奥斯的宫殿的过程经过了瑙西卡的精心安排，这与他日后的追述大不相同。尤利西斯在瑙西卡和侍女面前谨慎谦恭，请读者思考一下尤利西斯这样做的原因。本卷展现了一些古代社会生活的习俗，比如人们如何使用橄榄油、装酒时使用什么容器等，这些细节描述生动地展现了古希腊人的日常生活，值得在阅读时多加留意。

选文

SELECTION

So here Ulysses slept, overcome by sleep and toil; but Minerva went off to the country and city of the Phaeacians—a people who used to live in the fair town of Hypereia, near the lawless Cyclopes. Now the Cyclopes were stronger than they and plundered them, so their king Nausithous moved them thence and settled them in Scheria, far from all other people. He surrounded the city with a wall, built houses and temples, and divided the lands among his people; but he was dead and gone to the house of Hades, and King Alcinous, whose counsels were inspired of heaven, was now reigning. To his house, then, did Minerva hie in furtherance of the return of Ulysses.

She went straight to the beautifully decorated bedroom in which there slept a girl who was as lovely as a goddess, Nausicaa, daughter to King Alcinous. Two maid servants were sleeping near her, both very pretty, one on either side of the doorway, which was closed with well made folding doors. Minerva took the form of the famous sea captain Dymas's daughter, who was a bosom friend of Nausicaa and just her own age; then, coming up to the girl's bedside like a breath of wind, she hovered over her head and said:

"Nausicaa, what can your mother have been about, to have such a lazy daughter? Here are your clothes all lying in disorder, yet you are going to be married almost immediately, and should not only be well dressed yourself, but should find good clothes for those who attend you. This is the way to get yourself a good name, and to make your father and mother proud of you. Suppose, then, that we make tomorrow a washing day, and start at daybreak. I will come and help you so that you may have everything ready as soon as possible, for all the best young men among your own people are courting you, and you are not going to remain a maid much longer. Ask your father, therefore, to have a waggon and mules ready for us at daybreak, to take the rugs, robes, and girdles, and you can ride, too, which will be much pleasanter for you than walking, for the washing-cisterns are some way from the town."

When she had said this Minerva went away to Olympus, which they say is the everlasting home of the gods. Here no wind beats roughly, and neither rain nor snow can fall; but it abides in everlasting sunshine and in a great peacefulness of light, wherein the blessed gods are illumined for ever and ever. This was the place to which the goddess went when she had given instructions to the girl.

By and by morning came and woke Nausicaa, who began wondering about her dream; she therefore went to the other end of the house to tell her father and mother all about it, and found them in their own room. Her mother was sitting by the fireside spinning her purple yarn with her maids around her, and she happened to catch her father just as he was going out to attend a meeting of the town council, which the Phaeacian aldermen had convened. She stopped him and said:

"Papa dear, could you manage to let me have a good big waggon? I want to take all our dirty clothes to the river and wash them. You are the chief man here, so it is only right that you should have a clean shirt when you attend meetings of the council. Moreover, you have five sons at home, two of them married, while the other three are good looking bachelors; you know they always like to have clean linen when they go to a dance, and I have been thinking about all this."

She did not say a word about her own wedding, for she did not like to, but her father knew and said, "You shall have the mules, my love, and whatever else you have a mind for. Be off with you, and the men shall get you a good strong waggon with a body to it that will hold you're your clothes."

On this he gave his orders to the servants, who got the waggon out, harnessed the mules, and put them to, while the girl brought the clothes down from the linen room and placed them on the waggon. Her mother prepared her a basket of provisions with all sorts of good things, and a goat skin full of wine; the girl now got into the waggon, and her mother gave her also a golden cruse of oil, that she and her women might anoint themselves. Then she took the whip and reins and lashed the mules on, whereon they set off, and their hoofs clattered on the road. They pulled without flagging, and carried not only Nausicaa and her wash of clothes, but the maids also who were with her.

When they reached the water side they went to the washing cisterns, through which there ran at all times enough pure water to wash any quantity of linen, no matter how dirty. Here they unharnessed the mules and turned them out to feed on the sweet juicy herbage that grew by the water side. They took the clothes out of the waggon, put them in the water, and vied with one another in treading them in the pits to get the dirt out. After they had washed them and got them quite clean, they laid them out by the sea side, where the waves had raised a high beach of shingle, and set about washing themselves and anointing themselves with olive oil. Then they got their dinner by the side of the stream, and waited for the sun to finish drying the clothes. When they had done dinner they threw off the veils that covered their heads and began to play at ball, while Nausicaa sang for them. As the huntress Diana goes forth upon the mountains of Taygetus or Erymanthus to hunt wild boars or deer, and the wood nymphs, daughters of Aegis-bearing Jove, take their sport along with her (then is Leto proud at seeing her daughter stand a full head taller than the others, and eclipse the loveliest amid a whole bevy of beauties), even so did the girl outshine her handmaids.

When it was time for them to start home, and they were folding the clothes and putting them into the waggon, Minerva began to consider how Ulysses should wake up and see the handsome girl who was to conduct him to the city of the Phaeacians. The girl, therefore, threw a ball at one of the maids, which missed her and fell into deep water. On this they all shouted, and the noise they made woke Ulysses, who sat up in his bed of leaves and began to wonder what it might all be.

"Alas," said he to himself, "what kind of people have I come amongst? Are they cruel, savage, and uncivilised, or hospitable and humane? I seem to hear the voices of young women, and they sound like those of the nymphs that haunt mountain tops, or springs of rivers and meadows of green grass. At any rate I am among a race of men and women. Let me try if I cannot manage to get a look at them."

As he said this he crept from under his bush, and broke off a bough covered with thick leaves to hide his nakedness. He looked like some lion of the wilderness that stalks about exulting in his strength and defying both wind and rain; his eyes glare as he prowls in quest of oxen, sheep, or deer, for he is famished, and will dare break even into a well fenced homestead, trying to get at the sheep—even such did Ulysses seem to the young women, as he drew near to them all naked as he was, for he was in great want. On seeing one so unkempt and so begrimed with salt water, the others scampered off along the spits that jutted out into the sea, but the daughter of Alcinous stood firm, for Minerva put courage into her heart and took away all fear from her. She stood right in front of Ulysses, and he doubted whether he should go up to her, throw himself at her feet, and embrace her knees as a suppliant, or stay where he was and entreat her to give him some clothes and show him the way to the town. In the end he deemed it best to entreat her from a distance in case the girl should take offence at his coming near enough to clasp her knees, so he addressed her in honeyed and persuasive language.

"O queen," he said, "I implore your aid—but tell me, are you a goddess or are you a mortal woman? If you are a goddess and dwell in heaven, I can only conjecture that you are Jove's daughter Diana, for your face and figure resemble none but hers; if on the other hand you are a mortal and live on earth, thrice happy are your father and mother—thrice happy, too, are your brothers and sisters; how proud and delighted they must feel when they see so fair a scion as yourself going out to a dance; most happy, however, of all will he be whose wedding gifts have been the richest, and who takes you to his own home. I never yet saw any one so beautiful, neither man nor woman, and am lost in admiration as I behold you. I can only compare you to a young palm tree which I saw when I was at Delos[1] growing near the altar of Apollo—for I was there, too, with much people after me, when I was on that journey which has been the source of all my troubles. Never yet did such a young plant shoot out of the ground as that was, and I admired and wondered at it exactly as I now admire and wonder at yourself. I dare not clasp your knees, but I am in great distress; yesterday made the twentieth day that I had been tossing about upon the sea. The winds and waves have taken me all the way from the Ogygian island, and now fate has flung me upon this coast that I may endure still further suffering; for I do not think that I have yet come to the end of it, but rather that heaven has still much evil in store for me.

"And now, O queen, have pity upon me, for you are the first person I have met, and I

---

1 Delos 是阿波罗（Apollo）的出生地。

know no one else in this country. Show me the way to your town, and let me have anything that you may have brought hither to wrap your clothes in. May heaven grant you in all things your heart's desire—husband, house, and a happy, peaceful home; for there is nothing better in this world than that man and wife should be of one mind in a house. It discomfits their enemies, makes the hearts of their friends glad, and they themselves know more about it than any one."

To this Nausicaa answered, "Stranger, you appear to be a sensible, well-disposed person. There is no accounting for luck; Jove gives prosperity to rich and poor just as he chooses, so you must take what he has seen fit to send you, and make the best of it. Now, however, that you have come to this our country, you shall not want for clothes nor for anything else that a foreigner in distress may reasonably look for. I will show you the way to the town, and will tell you the name of our people; we are called Phaeacians, and I am daughter to Alcinous, in whom the whole power of the state is vested."

Then she called her maids and said, "Stay where you are, you girls. Can you not see a man without running away from him? Do you take him for a robber or a murderer? Neither he nor any one else can come here to do us Phaeacians any harm, for we are dear to the gods, and live apart on a land's end that juts into the sounding sea, and have nothing to do with any other people. This is only some poor man who has lost his way, and we must be kind to him, for strangers and foreigners in distress are under Jove's protection, and will take what they can get and be thankful; so, girls, give the poor fellow something to eat and drink, and wash him in the stream at some place that is sheltered from the wind."

On this the maids left off running away and began calling one another back. They made Ulysses sit down in the shelter as Nausicaa had told them, and brought him a shirt and cloak. They also brought him the little golden cruse of oil, and told him to go and wash in the stream. But Ulysses said, "Young women, please to stand a little on one side that I may wash the brine from my shoulders and anoint myself with oil, for it is long enough since my skin has had a drop of oil upon it. I cannot wash as long as you all keep standing there. I am ashamed to strip before a number of good looking young women."

Then they stood on one side and went to tell the girl, while Ulysses washed himself in the stream and scrubbed the brine from his back and from his broad shoulders. When he had thoroughly washed himself, and had got the brine out of his hair, he anointed himself with oil, and put on the clothes which the girl had given him; Minerva then made him look taller and stronger than before, she also made the hair grow thick on the top of his head, and flow down in curls like hyacinth blossoms; she glorified him about the head and shoulders as a skilful workman who has studied art of all kinds under Vulcan and Minerva[1] enriches a piece of silver plate by gilding it—and his work is full of beauty. Then he went and sat down a little way off upon the beach, looking quite young and handsome, and the girl gazed on him with admiration; then she said to her maids:

"Hush, my dears, for I want to say something. I believe the gods who live in heaven have sent this man to the Phaeacians. When I first saw him I thought him plain, but now his appearance is like that of the gods who dwell in heaven. I should like my future husband to be just such another as he is, if he would only stay here and not want to go away. However, give him something to eat and drink."

They did as they were told, and set food before Ulysses, who ate and drank ravenously, for it was long since he had had food of any kind. Meanwhile, Nausicaa bethought her of another matter. She got the linen folded and placed in the waggon, she then yoked the mules, and, as she took her seat, she called Ulysses:

"Stranger," said she, "rise and let us be going back to the town; I will introduce you at the house of my excellent father, where I can tell you that you will meet all the best people among the Phaeacians. But be sure and do as I bid you, for you seem to be a sensible person. As long as we are going past the fields and farm lands, follow briskly behind the waggon along with the maids and I will lead the way myself. Presently, however, we shall come to the town, where you will find a high wall running all round it, and a good harbour on either side with a narrow entrance into the city, and the ships will be drawn up by the road side, for every one has a place where his own ship can lie. You will see the market place with a temple of Neptune in the middle of it, and paved with large stones bedded in the earth. Here people deal in ship's gear of all kinds, such as cables and sails, and here, too, are the places where oars are made, for the Phaeacians are not a nation of archers; they know nothing about bows and arrows, but are a sea-faring folk, and pride themselves on their masts, oars, and ships, with which they travel far over the sea.

"I am afraid of the gossip and scandal that may be set on foot against me later on; for the people here are very ill-natured, and some low fellow, if he met us, might say, 'Who is

---

1　Vulcan 和 Minerva 是希腊神话中掌管农业和手工业的神祇。

this fine-looking stranger that is going about with Nausicaa? Where did she find him? I suppose she is going to marry him. Perhaps he is a vagabond sailor whom she has taken from some foreign vessel, for we have no neighbours; or some god has at last come down from heaven in answer to her prayers, and she is going to live with him all the rest of her life. It would be a good thing if she would take herself off and find a husband somewhere else, for she will not look at one of the many excellent young Phaeacians who are in love with her.' This is the kind of disparaging remark that would be made about me, and I could not complain, for I should myself be scandalized at seeing any other girl do the like, and go about with men in spite of everybody, while her father and mother were still alive, and without having been married in the face of all the world.

"If, therefore, you want my father to give you an escort and to help you home, do as I bid you; you will see a beautiful grove of poplars by the road side dedicated to Minerva; it has a well in it and a meadow all round it. Here my father has a field of rich garden ground, about as far from the town as a man's voice will carry. Sit down there and wait for a while till the rest of us can get into the town and reach my father's house. Then, when you think we must have done this, come into the town and ask the way to the house of my father Alcinous. You will have no difficulty in finding it; any child will point it out to you, for no one else in the whole town has anything like such a fine house as he has. When you have got past the gates and through the outer court, go right across the inner court till you come to my mother. You will find her sitting by the fire and spinning her purple wool by firelight. It is a fine sight to see her as she leans back against one of the bearing-posts with her maids all ranged behind her. Close to her seat stands that of my father, on which he sits and topes like an immortal god. Never mind him, but go up to my mother, and lay your hands upon her knees if you would get home quickly. If you can gain her over, you may hope to see your own country again, no matter how distant it may be."

...[1]

(From Book VI)

---

1 此处省略瑙西卡带尤利西斯进城，尤利西斯向密涅瓦祈祷自己受到费埃克斯人（Phaeacians）欢迎的故事。

思考题

QUESTIONS

1 Dreams play a special role in Greek mythology and literature. Minerva appears in Nausicaa's dream as the book opens. What is the function of the dream as regards the plot? What is the possible relationship between dreams and reality in the epic?

2 Ancient Greece abounded with olives from which people pressed oil. What is olive oil used for as is described in this book?

3 Nausicaa goes out of the town to wash clothes. She takes wine with her. What container does she use to store the wine? This container is going to appear in later books. Pay attention to it.

4 What can you tell about Nausicaa's character from the way she deals with her father as well as Ulysses?

5 When Calypso talks about Ulysses' wife in jealousy, she mentions two good qualities that are expected of women. What are they? Does the Greek aesthetics change much from ours?

6 Ulysses "wonders" (Para. 10) and "doubts" (Para. 12) in his dealing with Nausicaa. What can we tell about his character?

7 What are the blessings Ulysses makes to Nausicaa? What values underlie the blessings? How do they relate to the theme of the epic?

8 Why doesn't Nausicaa herself take Ulysses to her father's house? What is people's expectation of and demand on a maiden girl's behavior?

第五章

国宴述往
技压群雄

导 读

INTRODUCTION

　　《奥德赛》第七卷中，尤利西斯被带入国王阿尔基诺奥斯的宫殿，受到了国王和王后的接待。本章选自第八卷，讲述了阿尔基诺奥斯设宴款待尤利西斯，席间尤利西斯两度听闻歌人吟唱特洛伊战争的故事，两度落泪。国王看到后问他原因，于是尤利西斯开始讲述自己的历险故事。在宴会后举行的竞技比赛中，尤利西斯接受挑战，在掷饼比赛中获得了胜利，也赢得了费埃克斯人的尊重。

　　本章展示了古代宴会的习俗。人们在聚会宴饮时往往要欣赏歌舞，本卷对歌人得摩多科斯的描述与荷马本人形象一致（二人都是吟唱英雄故事的眼盲的歌人）。宴会之后会举行体育竞赛，包括赛跑、掷饼、跳远、角力等，可见古希腊人极为热爱运动。阿尔基诺奥斯在完全不知道尤利西斯姓名来历的情况下就热情地款待他，赠送他珍贵的礼物，还答应护送他回家。这是古希腊人普遍遵行的待客之道。在第一章中，特勒马科斯也是这样招待密涅瓦的。

选文

SELECTION

...[1]

A servant presently led in the famous bard Demodocus, whom the muse[2] had dearly loved, but to whom she had given both good and evil, for though she had endowed him with a divine gift of song, she had robbed him of his eyesight. Pontonous set a seat for him among the guests, leaning it up against a bearing-post. He hung the lyre for him on a peg over his head, and showed him where he was to feel for it with his hands. He also set a fair table with a basket of victuals by his side, and a cup of wine from which he might drink whenever he was so disposed.

The company then laid their hands upon the good things that were before them, but as soon as they had had enough to eat and drink, the muse inspired Demodocus to sing the feats of heroes, and more especially a matter that was then in the mouths of all men, to wit, the quarrel between Ulysses and Achilles, and the fierce words that they heaped on one another as they sat together at a banquet. But Agamemnon was glad when he heard his chieftains quarrelling with one another, for Apollo had foretold him this at Pytho[3] when he

---

1 本卷开头是阿尔基诺奥斯（Alicinous）举行宴会款待尤利西斯。下面是对宴会的描写。

2 古希腊人认为歌人受到缪斯（muse）神启所以能唱。

3 Pytho 指的是得尔斐（Delphi），阿波罗著名的神庙即在此地。

crossed the stone floor to consult the oracle. Here was the beginning of the evil that by the will of Jove fell both upon Danaans and Trojans.

Thus sang the bard, but Ulysses drew his purple mantle over his head and covered his face, for he was ashamed to let the Phaeacians see that he was weeping. When the bard left off singing he wiped the tears from his eyes, uncovered his face, and, taking his cup, made a drink-offering to the gods; but when the Phaeacians pressed Demodocus to sing further, for they delighted in his lays, then Ulysses again drew his mantle over his head and wept bitterly. No one noticed his distress except Alcinous, who was sitting near him, and heard the heavy sighs that he was heaving. So he at once said, "Aldermen and town councillors of the Phaeacians, we have had enough now, both of the feast, and of the minstrelsy that is its due accompaniment; let us proceed therefore to the athletic sports, so that our guest on his return home may be able to tell his friends how much we surpass all other nations as boxers, wrestlers, jumpers, and runners."

...[1]

... Alcinous's son Laodamas was the best boxer, and he it was who presently said, when they had all been diverted with the games, "Let us ask the stranger whether he excels in any of these sports; he seems very powerfully built; his thighs, calves, hands, and neck are of prodigious strength, nor is he at all old, but he has suffered much lately, and there is nothing like the sea for making havoc with a man, no matter how strong he is."

"You are quite right, Laodamas," replied Euryalus, "go up to your guest and speak to him about it yourself."

When Laodamas heard this he made his way into the middle of the crowd and said to Ulysses, "I hope, Sir, that you will enter yourself for some one or other of our competitions if you are skilled in any of them—and you must have gone in for many a one before now. There is nothing that does any one so much credit all his life long as the showing himself a proper man with his hands and feet. Have a try therefore at something, and banish all sorrow from your mind. Your return home will not be long delayed, for the ship is already drawn into the water, and the crew is found."

Ulysses answered, "Laodamas, why do you taunt me in this way? My mind is set rather

---

1 此处省略众人走出宫殿，观看费埃克斯年轻人进行各项比赛的内容。

on cares than contests; I have been through infinite trouble, and am come among you now as a suppliant, praying your king and people to further me on my return home."

Then Euryalus reviled him outright and said, "I gather, then, that you are unskilled in any of the many sports that men generally delight in. I suppose you are one of those grasping traders that go about in ships as captains or merchants, and who think of nothing but of their outward freights and homeward cargoes. There does not seem to be much of the athlete about you."

"For shame, Sir," answered Ulysses, fiercely, "you are an insolent fellow—so true is it that the gods do not grace all men alike in speech, person, and understanding. One man may be of weak presence, but heaven has adorned this with such a good conversation that he charms every one who sees him; his honeyed moderation carries his hearers with him so that he is leader in all assemblies of his fellows, and wherever he goes he is looked up to. Another may be as handsome as a god, but his good looks are not crowned with discretion. This is your case. No god could make a finer looking fellow than you are, but you are a fool. Your ill-judged remarks have made me exceedingly angry, and you are quite mistaken, for I excel in a great many athletic exercises; indeed, so long as I had youth and strength, I was among the first athletes of the age. Now, however, I am worn out by labour and sorrow, for I have gone through much both on the field of battle and by the waves of the weary sea; still, in spite of all this I will compete, for your taunts have stung me to the quick."

So he hurried up without even taking his cloak off, and seized a disc, larger, more massive and much heavier than those used by the Phaeacians when disc-throwing among themselves. Then, swinging it back, he threw it from his brawny hand, and it made a humming sound in the air as he did so. The Phaeacians quailed beneath the rushing of its flight as it sped gracefully from his hand, and flew beyond any mark that had been made yet. Minerva, in the form of a man, came and marked the place where it had fallen. "A blind man, Sir," said she, "could easily tell your mark by groping for it—it is so far ahead of any other. You may make your mind easy about this contest, for no Phaeacian can come near to such a throw as yours."

Ulysses was glad when he found he had a friend among the lookers-on, so he began to speak more pleasantly. "Young men," said he, "come up to that throw if you can, and I will throw another disc as heavy or even heavier. If anyone wants to have a bout with me let him come on, for I am exceedingly angry; I will box, wrestle, or run, I do not care what it is, with any man of you all except Laodamas, but not with him because I am his guest, and one cannot compete with one's own personal friend. At least I do not think it a prudent or a sensible thing for a guest to challenge his host's family at any game, especially when he is in a foreign country. He will cut the ground from under his own feet if he does; but I make no exception as regards any one else, for I want to have the matter out and know which is the best man. I am a good hand at every kind of athletic sport known among mankind. I am an excellent archer. In battle I am always the first to bring a man down with my arrow, no matter how many more are taking aim at him alongside of me. Philoctetes[1] was the only man who could shoot better than I could when we Achaeans were before Troy and in practice. I far excel every one else in the whole world, of those who still eat bread upon the face of the earth, but I should not like to shoot against the mighty dead, such as Hercules, or Eurytus the Oechalian—men who could shoot against the gods themselves. This in fact was how Eurytus came prematurely by his end, for Apollo was angry with him and killed him because he challenged him as an archer. I can throw a dart farther than any one else can shoot an arrow. Running is the only point in respect of which I am afraid some of the Phaeacians might beat me, for I have been brought down very low at sea; my provisions ran short, and therefore I am still weak."

They all held their peace except King Alcinous, who began, "Sir, we have had much pleasure in hearing all that you have told us, from which I understand that you are willing to show your prowess, as having been displeased with some insolent remarks that have been made to you by one of our athletes, and which could never have been uttered by any one who knows how to talk with propriety. I hope you will apprehend my meaning, and will explain to any one of your chief men who may be dining with yourself and your family when you get home, that we have a hereditary aptitude for accomplishments of all kinds. We are not particularly remarkable for our boxing, nor yet as wrestlers, but we are singularly fleet of foot and are excellent sailors. We are extremely fond of good dinners, music, and dancing; we also like frequent changes of linen, warm baths, and good beds, so now, please, some of you who are the best dancers set about dancing, that our guest on his return home may be able to tell his friends how much we surpass all other nations as sailors, runners, dancers, and minstrels. Demodocus has left his lyre at my house, so run some one or other of you and fetch it for him."

---

1 Philoctetes 是著名的箭手，也参加了特洛伊战争。

...

Meanwhile the bard began to sing the loves of Mars and Venus, and how they first began their intrigue in the house of Vulcan. Mars made Venus many presents, and defiled King Vulcan's marriage bed, so the sun, who saw what they were about, told Vulcan. Vulcan was very angry when he heard such dreadful news, so he went to his smithy brooding mischief, got his great anvil into its place, and began to forge some chains which none could either unloose or break, so that they might stay there in that place. When he had finished his snare he went into his bedroom and festooned the bed-posts all over with chains like cobwebs; he also let many hang down from the great beam of the ceiling. Not even a god could see them so fine and subtle were they. As soon as he had spread the chains all over the bed, he made as though he were setting out for the fair state of Lemnos, which of all places in the world was the one he was most fond of. But Mars kept no blind look out, and as soon as he saw him start, hurried off to his house, burning with love for Venus.

Now Venus was just come in from a visit to her father Jove, and was about sitting down when Mars came inside the house, and said as he took her hand in his own, "Let us go to the couch of Vulcan: he is not at home, but is gone off to Lemnos among the Sintians, whose speech is barbarous."

She was nothing loth, so they went to the couch to take their rest, whereon they were caught in the toils which cunning Vulcan had spread for them, and could neither get up nor stir hand or foot, but found too late that they were in a trap. Then Vulcan came up to them, for he had turned back before reaching Lemnos, when his scout the sun told him what was going on. He was in a furious passion, and stood in the vestibule making a dreadful noise as he shouted to all the gods.

"Father Jove," he cried, "and all you other blessed gods who live for ever, come here and see the ridiculous and disgraceful sight that I will show you. Jove's daughter Venus is always dishonouring me because I am lame. She is in love with Mars, who is handsome and clean built, whereas I am a cripple—but my parents are to blame for that, not I; they ought never to have begotten me. Come and see the pair together asleep on my bed. It makes me furious to look at them. They are very fond of one another, but I do not think they will lie there longer than they can help, nor do I think that they will sleep much; there, however, they shall stay till her father has repaid me the sum I gave him for his baggage of a daughter, who is fair but not honest."

On this the gods gathered to the house of Vulcan. Earth-encircling Neptune came, and Mercury the bringer of luck, and King Apollo, but the goddesses staid at home all of them for shame. Then the givers of all good things stood in the doorway, and the blessed gods roared with inextinguishable laughter, as they saw how cunning Vulcan had been, whereon one would turn towards his neighbour saying:

"Ill deeds do not prosper, and the weak confound the strong. See how limping Vulcan, lame as he is, has caught Mars who is the fleetest god in heaven; and now Mars will be cast in heavy damages."

Thus did they converse, but King Apollo said to Mercury, "Messenger Mercury, giver of good things, you would not care how strong the chains were, would you, if you could sleep with Venus?"

"King Apollo," answered Mercury, "I only wish I might get the chance, though there were three times as many chains—and you might look on, all of you, gods and goddesses, but I would sleep with her if I could."

...

Thus sang the bard, and both Ulysses and the seafaring Phaeacians were charmed as they heard him.

Then Alcinous told Laodamas and Halius to dance alone, for there was no one to compete with them. So they took a red ball which Polybus had made for them, and one of them bent himself backwards and threw it up towards the clouds, while the other jumped from off the ground and caught it with ease before it came down again. When they had done throwing the ball straight up into the air they began to dance, and at the same time kept on throwing it backwards and forwards to one another, while all the young men in the ring applauded and made a great stamping with their feet. Then Ulysses said:

"King Alcinous, you said your people were the nimblest dancers in the world, and indeed they have proved themselves to be so. I was astonished as I saw them."

The king was delighted at this, and exclaimed to the Phaeacians, "Aldermen and town councillors, our guest seems to be a person of singular judgement; let us give him such proof of our hospitality as he may reasonably expect. There are twelve chief men among you, and counting myself there are thirteen; contribute, each of you, a clean cloak, a shirt, and a talent of fine gold; let us give him all this in a lump down at once, so that when he gets his supper he may do so with a light heart. As for Euryalus he will have to make a formal apology and a present too, for he has been rude."

Thus did he speak. The others all of them applauded his saying, and sent their servants to fetch the presents. Then Euryalus said, "King Alcinous, I will give the stranger all the satisfaction you require. He shall have my sword, which is of bronze, all but the hilt, which is of silver. I will also give him the scabbard of newly sawn ivory into which it fits. It will be worth a great deal to him."

As he spoke he placed the sword in the hands of Ulysses and said, "Good luck to you, father stranger; if anything has been said amiss may the winds blow it away with them, and may heaven grant you a safe return, for I understand you have been long away from home, and have gone through much hardship."

To which Ulysses answered, "Good luck to you too my friend, and may the gods grant you every happiness. I hope you will not miss the sword you have given me along with your apology."

With these words he girded the sword about his shoulders and towards sun down the presents began to make their appearance, as the servants of the donors kept bringing them to the house of King Alcinous; here his sons received them, and placed them under their mother's charge. Then Alcinous led the way to the house and bade his guests take their seats.

"Wife," said he, turning to Queen Arete, "Go, fetch the best chest we have, and put a clean cloak and shirt in it. Also, set a copper on the fire and heat some water; our guest will take a warm bath; see also to the careful packing of the presents that the noble Phaeacians have made him; he will thus better enjoy both his supper and the singing that will follow. I shall myself give him this golden goblet—which is of exquisite workmanship—that he may be reminded of me for the rest of his life whenever he makes a drink offering to Jove, or to any of the gods."

Then Arete told her maids to set a large tripod upon the fire as fast as they could, whereon they set a tripod full of bath water on to a clear fire; they threw on sticks to make it blaze, and the water became hot as the flame played about the belly of the tripod. Meanwhile Arete brought a magnificent chest from her own room, and inside it she packed all the beautiful presents of gold and raiment which the Phaeacians had brought. Lastly she added a cloak and a good shirt from Alcinous, and said to Ulysses:

"See to the lid yourself, and have the whole bound round at once, for fear any one should rob you by the way when you are asleep in your ship."

When Ulysses heard this he put the lid on the chest and made it fast with a bond that Circe[1] had taught him. He had done so before an upper servant told him to come to the bath and wash himself. He was very glad of a warm bath, for he had had no one to wait upon him ever since he left the house of Calypso, who as long as he remained with her had taken as good care of him as though he had been a god. When the servants had done washing and anointing him with oil, and had given him a clean cloak and shirt, he left the bath room and joined the guests who were sitting over their wine. Lovely Nausicaa stood by one of the bearing-posts supporting the roof of the cloister, and admired him as she saw him pass. "Farewell stranger," said she, "do not forget me when you are safe at home again, for it is to me first that you owe a ransom for having saved your life."

And Ulysses said, "Nausicaa, daughter of great Alcinous, may Jove the mighty husband of Juno, grant that I may reach my home; so shall I bless you as my guardian angel all my days, for it was you who saved me."

When he had said this, he seated himself beside Alcinous. Supper was then served, and the wine was mixed for drinking. A servant led in the favourite bard Demodocus, and set him in the midst of the company, near one of the bearing-posts supporting the cloister, that he might lean against it. Then Ulysses cut off a piece of roast pork with plenty of fat (for there was abundance left on the joint) and said to a servant, "Take this piece of pork over to Demodocus and tell him to eat it; for all the pain his lays may cause me I will salute him none the less; bards are honoured and respected throughout the world, for the muse teaches them their songs and loves them."

The servant carried the pork in his fingers over to Demodocus, who took it and was very much pleased. They then laid their hands on the good things that were before them, and as soon as they had had to eat and drink, Ulysses said to Demodocus, "Demodocus, there is no one in the world whom I admire more than I do you. You must have studied under the Muse, Jove's daughter, and under Apollo, so accurately do you sing the return of the Achaeans with all their sufferings and adventures. If you were not there yourself, you must have heard it all from some one who was. Now, however, change your song and tell us of the wooden horse

---

1　基尔克（Circe）是尤利西斯回家途中遇到的魔女，第七章又会讲到她的故事。

which Epeus made with the assistance of Minerva, and which Ulysses got by stratagem into the fort of Troy after freighting it with the men who afterwards sacked the city. If you will sing this tale aright I will tell all the world how magnificently heaven has endowed you."

The bard inspired of heaven took up the story at the point where some of the Argives set fire to their tents and sailed away while others, hidden within the horse, were waiting with Ulysses in the Trojan place of assembly. For the Trojans themselves had drawn the horse into their fortress, and it stood there while they sat in council round it, and were in three minds as to what they should do. Some were for breaking it up then and there; others would have it dragged to the top of the rock on which the fortress stood, and then thrown down the precipice; while yet others were for letting it remain as an offering and propitiation for the gods. And this was how they settled it in the end, for the city was doomed when it took in that horse, within which were all the bravest of the Argives waiting to bring death and destruction on the Trojans. Anon he sang how the sons of the Achaeans issued from the horse, and sacked the town, breaking out from their ambuscade. He sang how they overran the city hither and thither and ravaged it, and how Ulysses went raging like Mars along with Menelaus to the house of Deiphobus[1]. It was there that the fight raged most furiously, nevertheless by Minerva's help he was victorious.

All this he told, but Ulysses was overcome as he heard him, and his cheeks were wet with tears. He wept as a woman weeps when she throws herself on the body of her husband who has fallen before his own city and people, fighting bravely in defence of his home and children. She screams aloud and flings her arms about him as he lies gasping for breath and dying, but her enemies beat her from behind about the back and shoulders, and carry her off into slavery, to a life of labour and sorrow, and the beauty fades from her cheeks—even so piteously did Ulysses weep, but none of those present perceived his tears except Alcinous, who was sitting near him, and could hear the sobs and sighs that he was heaving. The king, therefore, at once rose and said:

"Aldermen and town councillors of the Phaeacians, let Demodocus cease his song, for there are those present who do not seem to like it. From the moment that we had done supper and Demodocus began to sing, our guest has been all the time groaning and lamenting. He is evidently in great trouble, so let the bard leave off, that we may all

---

1　Deiphobus 是特洛伊王子。

enjoy ourselves, hosts and guest alike. This will be much more as it should be, for all these festivities, with the escort and the presents that we are making with so much good will are wholly in his honour, and any one with even a moderate amount of right feeling knows that he ought to treat a guest and a suppliant as though he were his own brother.

"Therefore, Sir, do you on your part affect no more concealment nor reserve in the matter about which I shall ask you; it will be more polite in you to give me a plain answer; tell me the name by which your father and mother over yonder used to call you, and by which you were known among your neighbours and fellow-citizens. There is no one, neither rich nor poor, who is absolutely without any name whatever, for people's fathers and mothers give them names as soon as they are born. Tell me also your country, nation, and city, that our ships may shape their purpose accordingly and take you there. For the Phaeacians have no pilots; their vessels have no rudders as those of other nations have, but the ships themselves understand what it is that we are thinking about and want; they know all the cities and countries in the whole world, and can traverse the sea just as well even when it is covered with mist and cloud, so that there is no danger of being wrecked or coming to any harm. Still I do remember hearing my father say that Neptune was angry with us for being too easy-going in the matter of giving people escorts. He said that one of these days he should wreck a ship of ours as it was returning from having escorted some one, and bury our city under a high mountain. This is what my father used to say, but whether the god will carry out his threat or no is a matter which he will decide for himself.

"And now, tell me and tell me true. Where have you been wandering, and in what countries have you travelled? Tell us of the peoples themselves, and of their cities—who were hostile, savage and uncivilised, and who, on the other hand, hospitable and humane. Tell us also why you are made so unhappy on hearing about the return of the Argive Danaans from Troy. The gods arranged all this, and sent them their misfortunes in order that future generations might have something to sing about. Did you lose some brave kinsman of your wife's when you were before Troy? A son-in-law or father-in-law—which are the nearest relations a man has outside his own flesh and blood? Or was it some brave and kindly-natured comrade—for a good friend is as dear to a man as his own brother?"

(From Book VIII)

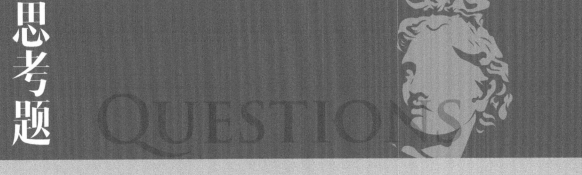

思考题

1. What do the Greeks usually do at a banquet?

2. Euryalus reviles Ulysses as a trader. What's the possible status of traders, compared with athletes?

3. Pay attention to the description of the bard and the way he is treated. Is he respected by the Phaeacians?

4. What are the other characteristics of the Phaeacians shown in this book?

5. Describe the guest-friendship the Phaeacians have for Ulysses.

6. Twice Ulysses hears Demodocus sing about the Trojan war and twice he sheds tears. Why? Does anyone notice him weeping?

7. What qualities do you find about Ulysses at sports?

8. What does the story of Venus and Mars tell us about gods and their moral stand on extramarital affairs?

第六章

独眼巨人
愤怒海神

本章主要节选自《奥德赛》第九卷。在本卷中尤利西斯向费埃克斯人表明了真实身份，开始讲述特洛伊战争后他在回家路上的冒险经历。节选的这部分除了在洛托法戈伊人国土上的历险之外，最主要的内容是尤利西斯与独眼巨人库克洛普斯的遭遇。尤利西斯和同伴不慎被库克洛普斯囚禁在洞穴中，六个同伴相继被库克洛普斯生吃。尤利西斯先用酒把库克洛普斯灌醉，然后刺瞎了他唯一的眼睛，再藏在羊肚子下逃出了洞穴。不料库克洛普斯是海神尼普顿的儿子，海神因为儿子被刺瞎而愤怒地展开了报复，尤利西斯从此开始了不幸的海上旅程。

　　剥开神话的外衣，我们可以看到，尤利西斯与库克洛普斯的冲突其实是一场尖锐的文化冲突，具体表现在政治、经济、信仰、风俗习惯等各个方面。库克洛普斯误以为"无人"是尤利西斯的名字，却忘记了"无人"这个词语本身的真实含义，这是犯了唯名论的错误。此外，尤利西斯对库克洛普斯居住的岛屿旁边的各岛情况描述得颇为详细，显示出一个老练的殖民者的眼光，由此可见海外殖民行为在古希腊普遍而重要。

选文

SELECTION

And Ulysses answered, "King Alcinous, it is a good thing to hear a bard with such a divine voice as this man has. There is nothing better or more delightful than when a whole people make merry together, with the guests sitting orderly to listen, while the table is loaded with bread and meats, and the cup-bearer draws wine and fills his cup for every man. This is indeed as fair a sight as a man can see. Now, however, since you are inclined to ask the story of my sorrows, and rekindle my own sad memories in respect of them, I do not know how to begin, nor yet how to continue and conclude my tale, for the hand of heaven has been laid heavily upon me.

"Firstly, then, I will tell you my name that you too may know it, and one day, if I outlive this time of sorrow, may become my guests though I live so far away from all of you. I am Ulysses son of Laertes, renowned among mankind for all manner of subtlety, so that my fame ascends to heaven. I live in Ithaca, where there is a high mountain called Neritum, covered with forests; and not far from it there is a group of islands very near to one another—Dulichium, Same, and the wooded island of Zacynthus. It lies squat on the horizon, all highest up in the sea towards the sunset, while the others lie away from it towards dawn. It is a rugged island, but it breeds brave men, and my eyes know none that they better love to look upon. The goddess Calypso kept me with her in her cave, and wanted me to marry her, as did also the cunning Aeaean[1] goddess Circe; but they could neither of them persuade me, for there is nothing dearer to a man than his own country and his parents, and however splendid a home he may have in a foreign country, if it be far from father or mother, he does not care about it. Now, however, I will tell you of the many hazardous adventures which by Jove's will I met with on my return from Troy.

...[2]

"I was driven thence by foul winds for a space of nine days upon the sea, but on the tenth day we reached the land of the Lotus-eaters, who live on a food that comes from a kind of flower. Here we landed to take in fresh water, and our crews got their mid-day meal on the shore near the ships. When they had eaten and drunk I sent two of my company to see what manner of men the people of the place might be, and they had a third man under them. They started at once, and went about among the Lotus-eaters, who did them no hurt, but gave them to eat of the lotus, which was so delicious that those who ate of it left off caring about home, and did not even want to go back and say what had happened to them, but were for staying and munching lotus with the Lotus-eaters without thinking further of their return; nevertheless, though they wept bitterly I forced them back to the ships and made them fast under the benches. Then I told the rest to go on board at once, lest any of them should taste of the lotus and leave off wanting to get home, so they took their places and smote the grey sea with their oars.

"We sailed hence, always in much distress, till we came to the land of the lawless and inhuman Cyclopes. Now the Cyclopes neither plant nor plough, but trust in providence, and live on such wheat, barley, and grapes as grow wild without any kind of tillage, and their wild grapes yield them wine as the sun and the rain may grow them. They have no laws nor assemblies of the people, but live in caves on the tops of high mountains; each is lord and master in his family, and they take no account of their neighbours.

"Now off their harbour there lies a wooded and fertile island not quite close to the land of the Cyclopes, but still not far. It is over-run with wild goats, that breed there in great numbers and are never disturbed by foot of man; for sportsmen—who as a rule will suffer so much hardship in forest or among mountain precipices—do not go there, nor yet again

---

1　Aeaea 是基尔克居住的岛屿。

2　尤利西斯开始讲述他离开特洛伊之后的历险。

is it ever ploughed or fed down, but it lies a wilderness untilled and unsown from year to year, and has no living thing upon it but only goats. For the Cyclopes have no ships, nor yet shipwrights who could make ships for them; they cannot therefore go from city to city, or sail over the sea to one another's country as people who have ships can do; if they had had these they would have colonised the island, for it is a very good one, and would yield everything in due season. There are meadows that in some places come right down to the sea shore, well watered and full of luscious grass; grapes would do there excellently; there is level land for ploughing, and it would always yield heavily at harvest time, for the soil is deep. There is a good harbour where no cables are wanted, nor yet anchors, nor need a ship be moored, but all one has to do is to beach one's vessel and stay there till the wind becomes fair for putting out to sea again. At the head of the harbour there is a spring of clear water coming out of a cave, and there are poplars growing all round it.

"Here we entered, but so dark was the night that some god must have brought us in, for there was nothing whatever to be seen. A thick mist hung all round our ships; the moon was hidden behind a mass of clouds so that no one could have seen the island if he had looked for it, nor were there any breakers to tell us we were close in shore before we found ourselves upon the land itself; when, however, we had beached the ships, we took down the sails, went ashore and camped upon the beach till daybreak.

"When the child of morning, rosy-fingered Dawn appeared, we admired the island and wandered all over it, while the nymphs Jove's daughters roused the wild goats that we might get some meat for our dinner. On this we fetched our spears and bows and arrows from the ships, and dividing ourselves into three bands began to shoot the goats. Heaven sent us excellent sport; I had twelve ships with me, and each ship got nine goats, while my own ship had ten; thus through the livelong day to the going down of the sun we ate and drank our fill, and we had plenty of wine left, for each one of us had taken many jars full when we sacked the city of the Cicons, and this had not yet run out. While we were feasting we kept turning our eyes towards the land of the Cyclopes, which was hard by, and saw the smoke of their stubble fires. We could almost fancy we heard their voices and the bleating of their sheep and goats, but when the sun went down and it came on dark, we camped down upon the beach, and next morning I called a council.

"'Stay here, my brave fellows,' said I, 'all the rest of you, while I go with my ship and exploit these people myself: I want to see if they are uncivilised savages, or a hospitable and humane race.'

"I went on board, bidding my men to do so also and loose the hawsers; so they took their places and smote the grey sea with their oars. When we got to the land, which was not far, there, on the face of a cliff near the sea, we saw a great cave overhung with laurels. It was a station for a great many sheep and goats, and outside there was a large yard, with a high wall round it made of stones built into the ground and of trees both pine and oak. This was the abode of a huge monster who was then away from home shepherding his flocks. He would have nothing to do with other people, but led the life of an outlaw. He was a horrid creature, not like a human being at all, but resembling rather some crag that stands out boldly against the sky on the top of a high mountain.

"I told my men to draw the ship ashore, and stay where they were, all but the twelve best among them, who were to go along with myself. I also took a goatskin of sweet black wine which had been given me by Maron, son of Euanthes, who was priest of Apollo the patron god of Ismarus, and lived within the wooded precincts of the temple. When we were sacking the city we respected him, and spared his life, as also his wife and child; so he made me some presents of great value—seven talents of fine gold, and a bowl of silver, with twelve jars of sweet wine, unblended, and of the most exquisite flavour. Not a man nor maid in the house knew about it, but only himself, his wife, and one housekeeper: when he drank it he mixed twenty parts of water to one of wine, and yet the fragrance from the mixing-bowl was so exquisite that it was impossible to refrain from drinking. I filled a large skin with this wine, and took a wallet full of provisions with me, for my mind misgave me that I might have to deal with some savage who would be of great strength, and would respect neither right nor law.

"We soon reached his cave, but he was out shepherding, so we went inside and took stock of all that we could see. His cheese-racks were loaded with cheeses, and he had more lambs and kids than his pens could hold. They were kept in separate flocks; first there were the hoggets, then the oldest of the younger lambs and lastly the very young ones all kept apart from one another; as for his dairy, all the vessels, bowls, and milk pails into which he milked, were swimming with whey. When they saw all this, my men begged me to let them first steal some cheeses, and make off with them to the ship; they would then return, drive down the lambs and kids, put them on board and sail away with them. It would have been indeed better if we had done so but I would not listen to them, for I wanted to see the owner himself, in the hope that he might give me a present. When, however, we saw him my poor men found him ill to deal with.

"We lit a fire, offered some of the cheeses in sacrifice, ate others of them, and then sat waiting till the Cyclops should come in with his sheep. When he came, he brought in with him a huge load of dry firewood to light the fire for his supper, and this he flung with such a noise on to the floor of his cave that we hid ourselves for fear at the far end of the cavern. Meanwhile he drove all the ewes inside, as well as the she-goats that he was going to milk, leaving the males, both rams and he-goats, outside in the yards. Then he rolled a huge stone to the mouth of the cave—so huge that two and twenty strong four-wheeled waggons would not be enough to draw it from its place against the doorway. When he had so done he sat down and milked his ewes and goats, all in due course, and then let each of them have her own young. He curdled half the milk and set it aside in wicker strainers, but the other half he poured into bowls that he might drink it for his supper. When he had got through with all his work, he lit the fire, and then caught sight of us, whereon he said:

"'Strangers, who are you? Where do sail from? Are you traders, or do you sail the sea as rovers, with your hands against every man, and every man's hand against you?'

"We were frightened out of our senses by his loud voice and monstrous form, but I managed to say, 'We are Achaeans on our way home from Troy, but by the will of Jove, and stress of weather, we have been driven far out of our course. We are the people of Agamemnon, son of Atreus, who has won infinite renown throughout the whole world, by sacking so great a city and killing so many people. We therefore humbly pray you to show us some hospitality, and otherwise make us such presents as visitors may reasonably expect. May your excellency fear the wrath of heaven, for we are your suppliants, and Jove takes all respectable travellers under his protection, for he is the avenger of all suppliants and foreigners in distress.'

"To this he gave me but a pitiless answer, 'Stranger,' said he, 'you are a fool, or else you know nothing of this country. Talk to me, indeed, about fearing the gods or shunning their anger? We Cyclopes do not care about Jove or any of your blessed gods, for we are ever so much stronger than they. I shall not spare either yourself or your companions out of any regard for Jove, unless I am in the humour for doing so. And now tell me where you made your ship fast when you came on shore. Was it round the point, or is she lying straight off the land?'

"He said this to draw me out, but I was too cunning to be caught in that way, so I answered with a lie; 'Neptune,' said I, 'sent my ship on to the rocks at the far end of your country, and wrecked it. We were driven on to them from the open sea, but I and those who are with me escaped the jaws of death.'

"The cruel wretch vouchsafed me not one word of answer, but with a sudden clutch he gripped up two of my men at once and dashed them down upon the ground as though they had been puppies. Their brains were shed upon the ground, and the earth was wet with their blood. Then he tore them limb from limb and supped upon them. He gobbled them up like a lion in the wilderness, flesh, bones, marrow, and entrails, without leaving anything uneaten. As for us, we wept and lifted up our hands to heaven on seeing such a horrid sight, for we did not know what else to do; but when the Cyclops had filled his huge paunch, and had washed down his meal of human flesh with a drink of neat milk, he stretched himself full length upon the ground among his sheep, and went to sleep. I was at first inclined to seize my sword, draw it, and drive it into his vitals, but I reflected that if I did we should all certainly be lost, for we should never be able to shift the stone which the monster had put in front of the door. So we stayed sobbing and sighing where we were till morning came.

"When the child of morning, rosy-fingered dawn, appeared, he again lit his fire, milked his goats and ewes, all quite rightly, and then let each have her own young one; as soon as he had got through with all his work, he clutched up two more of my men, and began eating them for his morning's meal. Presently, with the utmost ease, he rolled the stone away from the door and drove out his sheep, but he at once put it back again—as easily as though he were merely clapping the lid on to a quiver full of arrows. As soon as he had done so he shouted, and cried 'Shoo, shoo,' after his sheep to drive them on to the mountain; so I was left to scheme some way of taking my revenge and covering myself with glory.

"In the end I deemed it would be the best plan to do as follows: The Cyclops had a great club which was lying near one of the sheep pens; it was of green olive wood, and he had cut it intending to use it for a staff as soon as it should be dry. It was so huge that we could only compare it to the mast of a twenty-oared merchant vessel of large burden, and able to venture out into open sea. I went up to this club and cut off about six feet of it; I then gave this piece to the men and told them to fine it evenly off at one end, which they proceeded to do, and lastly I brought it to a point myself, charring the end in the fire to make it harder. When I had done this I hid it under dung, which was lying about all over the cave, and told the men to cast lots which of them should venture along with myself to lift it and bore it into the monster's eye while he was asleep. The lot fell upon the very four whom I should have chosen, and I myself made five. In the evening the wretch came back from shepherding, and drove his flocks into the cave—this time driving them all inside, and not leaving any in the yards; I suppose some fancy must have taken him, or a god must have prompted him to do so. As soon as he had put the stone back to its place against the door, he sat down, milked his ewes and his goats all quite rightly, and then let each have her own young one; when he had got through with all this work, he gripped up two more of my men, and made his supper off them. So I went up to him with an ivy-wood bowl of black wine in my hands:

"'Look here, Cyclops,' said I, you have been eating a great deal of man's flesh, so take this and drink some wine, that you may see what kind of liquor we had on board my ship. I was bringing it to you as a drink-offering, in the hope that you would take compassion upon me and further me on my way home, whereas all you do is to go on ramping and raving most intolerably. You ought to be ashamed of yourself; how can you expect people to come see you any more if you treat them in this way?'

"He then took the cup and drank. He was so delighted with the taste of the wine that he begged me for another bowl full. 'Be so kind,' he said, 'as to give me some more, and tell me your name at once. I want to make you a present that you will be glad to have. We have wine even in this country, for our soil grows grapes and the sun ripens them, but this drinks like Nectar and Ambrosia all in one.'

"I then gave him some more; three times did I fill the bowl for him, and three times did he drain it without thought or heed; then, when I saw that the wine had got into his head, I said to him as plausibly as I could: 'Cyclops, you ask my name and I will tell it you; give me, therefore, the present you promised me; my name is Noman; this is what my father and mother and my friends have always called me.'

"But the cruel wretch said, 'Then I will eat all Noman's comrades before Noman himself, and will keep Noman for the last. This is the present that I will make him.'

"As he spoke he reeled, and fell sprawling face upwards on the ground. His great neck hung heavily backwards and a deep sleep took hold upon him. Presently he turned sick, and threw up both wine and the gobbets of human flesh on which he had been gorging, for he was very drunk. Then I thrust the beam of wood far into the embers to heat it, and encouraged my men lest any of them should turn faint-hearted. When the wood, green though it was, was about to blaze, I drew it out of the fire glowing with heat, and my men gathered round me, for heaven had filled their hearts with courage. We drove the sharp end of the beam into the monster's eye, and bearing upon it with all my weight I kept turning it round and round as though I were boring a hole in a ship's plank with an auger, which two men with a wheel and strap can keep on turning as long as they choose. Even thus did we bore the red hot beam into his eye, till the boiling blood bubbled all over it as we worked it round and round, so that the steam from the burning eyeball scalded his eyelids and eyebrows, and the roots of the eye sputtered in the fire. As a blacksmith plunges an axe or hatchet into cold water to temper it—for it is this that gives strength to the iron—and it makes a great hiss as he does so, even thus did the Cyclops' eye hiss round the beam of olive wood, and his hideous yells made the cave ring again. We ran away in a fright, but he plucked the beam all besmirched with gore from his eye, and hurled it from him in a frenzy of rage and pain, shouting as he did so to the other Cyclopes who lived on the bleak headlands near him; so they gathered from all quarters round his cave when they heard him crying, and asked what was the matter with him.

"'What ails you, Polyphemus,' said they, 'that you make such a noise, breaking the stillness of the night, and preventing us from being able to sleep? Surely no man is carrying off your sheep? Surely no man is trying to kill you either by fraud or by force?'

"But Polyphemus shouted to them from inside the cave, 'Noman is killing me by fraud; no man is killing me by force.'

"'Then,' said they, 'if no man is attacking you, you must be ill; when Jove makes people ill, there is no help for it, and you had better pray to your father Neptune.'

"Then they went away, and I laughed inwardly at the success of my clever stratagem, but the Cyclops, groaning and in an agony of pain, felt about with his hands till he found the stone and took it from the door; then he sat in the doorway and stretched his hands in front of it to catch anyone going out with the sheep, for he thought I might be foolish enough to attempt this.

"As for myself I kept on puzzling to think how I could best save my own life and those of my companions; I schemed and schemed, as one who knows that his life depends upon it, for the danger was very great. In the end I deemed that this plan would be the best; the male sheep were well grown, and carried a heavy black fleece, so I bound them noiselessly in threes together, with some of the withies on which the wicked monster used to sleep. There was to be a man under the middle sheep, and the two on either side were to cover him, so that there were three sheep to each man. As for myself there was a ram finer than any of the others, so I caught hold of him by the back, ensconced myself in the thick wool under his belly, and hung on patiently to his fleece, face upwards, keeping a firm hold on it all the time.

"Thus, then, did we wait in great fear of mind till morning came, but when the child of morning, rosy-fingered Dawn, appeared, the male sheep hurried out to feed, while the ewes remained bleating about the pens waiting to be milked, for their udders were full to bursting; but their master in spite of all his pain felt the backs of all the sheep as they stood upright, without being sharp enough to find out that the men were underneath their bellies. As the ram was going out, last of all, heavy with its fleece and with the weight of my crafty self, Polyphemus laid hold of it and said:

"'My good ram, what is it that makes you the last to leave my cave this morning? You are not wont to let the ewes go before you, but lead the mob with a run whether to flowery mead or bubbling fountain, and are the first to come home again at night; but now you lag last of all. Is it because you know your master has lost his eye, and are sorry because that wicked Noman and his horrid crew has got him down in his drink and blinded him? But I will have his life yet. If you could understand and talk, you would tell me where the wretch is hiding, and I would dash his brains upon the ground till they flew all over the cave. I should thus have some satisfaction for the harm this no-good Noman has done me.'

"As he spoke he drove the ram outside, but when we were a little way out from the cave and yards, I first got from under the ram's belly, and then freed my comrades; as for the sheep, which were very fat, by constantly heading them in the right direction we managed to drive them down to the ship. The crew rejoiced greatly at seeing those of us who had escaped death, but wept for the others whom the Cyclops had killed. However, I made signs to them by nodding and frowning that they were to hush their crying, and told them to get all the sheep on board at once and put out to sea; so they went aboard, took their places, and smote the grey sea with their oars. Then, when I had got as far out as my voice would reach, I began to jeer at the Cyclops.

"'Cyclops,' said I, 'you should have taken better measure of your man before eating up his comrades in your cave. You wretch, eat up your visitors in your own house? You might have known that your sin would find you out, and now Jove and the other gods have punished you.'

"He got more and more furious as he heard me, so he tore the top from off a high mountain, and flung it just in front of my ship so that it was within a little of hitting the end of the rudder. The sea quaked as the rock fell into it, and the wash of the wave it raised carried us back towards the mainland, and forced us towards the shore. But I snatched up a long pole and kept the ship off, making signs to my men by nodding my head, that they must row for their lives, whereon they laid out with a will. When we had got twice as far as we were before, I was for jeering at the Cyclops again, but the men begged and prayed of me to hold my tongue.

"'Do not,' they exclaimed, 'be mad enough to provoke this savage creature further; he has thrown one rock at us already which drove us back again to the mainland, and we made sure it had been the death of us; if he had then heard any further sound of voices he would have pounded our heads and our ship's timbers into a jelly with the rugged rocks he would have heaved at us, for he can throw them a long way.'

"But I would not listen to them, and shouted out to him in my rage, 'Cyclops, if any one asks you who it was that put your eye out and spoiled your beauty, say it was the valiant warrior Ulysses, son of Laertes, who lives in Ithaca.'

"On this he groaned, and cried out, 'Alas, alas, then the old prophecy about me is coming true. There was a prophet here, at one time, a man both brave and of great stature, Telemus son of Eurymus, who was an excellent seer, and did all the prophesying for the Cyclopes till he grew old; he told me that all this would happen to me some day, and said I should lose my sight by the hand of Ulysses. I have been all along expecting some one of imposing presence and superhuman strength, whereas he turns out to be a little insignificant weakling, who has managed to blind my eye by taking advantage of me in my drink; come here, then, Ulysses, that I may make you presents to show my hospitality, and urge Neptune to help you forward on your journey—for Neptune and I are father and son. He, if he so will, shall heal me, which no one else neither god nor man can do.'

"Then I said, 'I wish I could be as sure of killing you outright and sending you down to the house of Hades, as I am that it will take more than Neptune to cure that eye of yours.'

"On this he lifted up his hands to the firmament of heaven and prayed, saying, 'Hear me, great Neptune; if I am indeed your own true begotten son, grant that Ulysses may never reach his home alive; or if he must get back to his friends at last, let him do so late and in sore plight after losing all his men (let him reach his home in another man's ship and find trouble in his house).'

"Thus did he pray, and Neptune heard his prayer. Then he picked up a rock much larger than the first, swung it aloft and hurled it with prodigious force. It fell just short of the ship, but was within a little of hitting the end of the rudder. The sea quaked as the rock fell into it, and the wash of the wave it raised drove us onwards on our way towards the shore of the island.

"When at last we got to the island where we had left the rest of our ships, we found our comrades lamenting us, and anxiously awaiting our return. We ran our vessel upon the sands and got out of her on to the sea shore; we also landed the Cyclops' sheep, and divided them equitably amongst us so that none might have reason to complain. As for the ram, my companions agreed that I should have it as an extra share; so I sacrificed it on the sea shore, and burned its thigh bones to Jove, who is the lord of all. But he heeded not my sacrifice, and only thought how he might destroy both my ships and my comrades.

...

(From Book IX)

思考题

QUESTIONS

1 Although *The Odyssey* is an adventurous story, it does not show the story by action, but rather by tale. This is one of the differences between *The Odyssey* and *The Iliad*. Do you expect this way of story-telling in the epic?

2 What are the differences between Cyclopes and Ulysses in terms of politics, economy, religion and social customs?

3 What is the relationship between Ulysses and his men? Is it like the relationship between feudal monarch and his barons?

4 When and where does Ulysses manifest himself as the leader of his group?

5 Ulysses' story is told in the first person narrative. Do you believe his narration, especially in view of the fact that he has concealed his true identity from the Phaeacians?

6 Ulysses introduces himself to Cyclopes boasting the feat of Agamemnon. What can you tell about the values he holds?

7 Why does Ulysses tell Cyclopes his real name? What are the values behind the behavior?

8 The 19th-century British poet Alfred Tennyson wrote "The Lotus-Eaters", elaborating the scene in the book. Read the poem on the next page and tell how the poet understands the epic.

The Lotus-Eaters

By Alfred Tennyson

...

Branches they bore of that enchanted stem,

Laden with flower and fruit, whereof they gave

To each, but whoso did receive of them

And taste, to him the gushing of the wave

Far far away did seem to mourn and rave

On alien shores; and if his fellow spake,

His voice was thin, as voices from the grave;

And deep-asleep he seem'd, yet all awake,

And music in his ears his beating heart did make. (lines 28-36)

...

Why are we weigh'd upon with heaviness,

And utterly consumed with sharp distress,

While all things else have rest from weariness?

All things have rest: why should we toil alone,

We only toil, who are the first of things,

And make perpetual moan,

Still from one sorrow to another thrown;

Nor ever fold our wings,

And cease from wanderings,

Nor steep our brows in slumber's holy balm;

Nor harken what the inner spirit sings,

"There is no joy but calm!"

Why should we only toil, the roof and crown of things? (lines 57-69)

异质文明
风王魔女

导读

INTRODUCTION

本章选自《奥德赛》第十卷。尤利西斯一行人来到艾奥利埃岛，风王艾奥洛斯款待了他们，并送给尤利西斯一个装满狂风的皮囊，让他的归程一帆风顺。不料皮囊被同伴偷偷解开，尤利西斯一行再次被风暴蹂躏。后来他们又遭遇了莱斯特律戈涅斯人，不少同伴丧生，幸存者逃亡到魔女基尔克的岛屿。基尔克用魔药把尤利西斯的同伴变成了猪，幸好墨丘利赠送尤利西斯药草，使他免遭魔药之害。

本章讲述了尤利西斯的三次历险，占篇幅较大的是魔女基尔克的故事。纵观整部荷马史诗，希腊人从来不懂得魔法，也不会使用魔药。魔法和魔药是存在于古希腊人世界之外的异质文明的产物，使用魔法和魔药的无一例外都是外族人。尤利西斯在历险中遭遇的各色人等，有的像莱斯特律戈涅斯人那样蛮力过人，有的像基尔克一样擅长魔法，这也充分体现了古希腊文化与周边文化之间存在的"文明的冲突"以及古希腊人对这些异质文明的看法。

选文

SELECTION

"Thence we went on to the Aeolian island where lives Aeolus, son of Hippotas, dear to the immortal gods. It is an island that floats (as it were) upon the sea, iron bound with a wall that girds it. Now, Aeolus has six daughters and six lusty sons, so he made the sons marry the daughters, and they all live with their dear father and mother, feasting and enjoying every conceivable kind of luxury. All day long the atmosphere of the house is loaded with the savour of roasting meats till it groans again, yard and all; but by night they sleep on their well made bedsteads, each with his own wife between the blankets. These were the people among whom we had now come.

"Aeolus entertained me for a whole month asking me questions all the time about Troy, the Argive fleet, and the return of the Achaeans. I told him exactly how everything had happened, and when I said I must go, and asked him to further me on my way, he made no sort of difficulty, but set about doing so at once. Moreover, he flayed me a prime ox-hide to hold the ways of the roaring winds, which he shut up in the hide as in a sack—for Jove had made him captain over the winds, and he could stir or still each one of them according to his own pleasure. He put the sack in the ship and bound the mouth so tightly with a silver thread that not even a breath of a side-wind could blow from any quarter. The West Wind which was fair for us did he alone let blow as it chose; but it all came to nothing, for we were lost through our own folly.

"Nine days and nine nights did we sail, and on the tenth day our native land showed on the horizon. We got so close in that we could see the stubble fires burning, and I, being then dead beat, fell into a light sleep, for I had never let the rudder out of my own hands, that we might get home the faster. On this the men fell to talking among themselves, and said I was bringing back gold and silver in the sack that Aeolus had given me. 'Bless my heart,' would one turn to his neighbour, saying, 'how this man gets honoured and makes friends to whatever city or country he may go. See what fine prizes he is taking home from Troy, while we, who have travelled just as far as he has, come back with hands as empty as we set out with—and now Aeolus has given him ever so much more. Quick—let us see what it all is, and how much gold and silver there is in the sack he gave him.'

"Thus they talked and evil counsels prevailed. They loosed the sack, whereupon the wind flew howling forth and raised a storm that carried us weeping out to sea and away from our own country. Then I awoke, and knew not whether to throw myself into the sea or to live on and make the best of it; but I bore it, covered myself up, and lay down in the ship, while the men lamented bitterly as the fierce winds bore our fleet back to the Aeolian island.

"When we reached it we went ashore to take in water, and dined hard by the ships. Immediately after dinner I took a herald and one of my men and went straight to the house of Aeolus, where I found him feasting with his wife and family; so we sat down as suppliants on the threshold. They were astounded when they saw us and said, 'Ulysses, what brings you here? What god has been ill-treating you? We took great pains to further you on your way home to Ithaca, or wherever it was that you wanted to go to.'

"Thus did they speak, but I answered sorrowfully, 'My men have undone me; they, and cruel sleep, have ruined me. My friends, mend me this mischief, for you can if you will.'

"I spoke as movingly as I could, but they said nothing, till their father answered, 'Vilest of mankind, get you gone at once out of the island; him whom heaven hates will I in no wise help. Be off, for you come here as one abhorred of heaven.' And with these words he sent me sorrowing from his door.

"Thence we sailed sadly on till the men were worn out with long and fruitless rowing, for there was no longer any wind to help them. Six days, night and day did we toil, and on the seventh day we reached the rocky stronghold of Lamus—Telepylus, the city of the Laestrygonians, where the shepherd who is driving in his sheep and goats [to be milked] salutes him who is driving out his flock [to feed] and this last answers the salute. In that country a man who could do without sleep might earn double wages, one as a herdsman of cattle, and another as a shepherd, for they work much the same by night as they do by day.

"When we reached the harbour we found it land-locked under steep cliffs, with a narrow entrance between two headlands. My captains took all their ships inside, and made them fast close to one another, for there was never so much as a breath of wind inside, but it was always dead calm. I kept my own ship outside, and moored it to a rock at the very end of the point; then I climbed a high rock to reconnoitre, but could see no sign neither of man nor cattle, only some smoke rising from the ground. So I sent two of my company with an attendant to find out what sort of people the inhabitants were.

"The men when they got on shore followed a level road by which the people draw their firewood from the mountains into the town, till presently they met a young woman who had come outside to fetch water, and who was daughter to a Laestrygonian named Antiphates. She was going to the fountain Artacia from which the people bring in their water, and when my men had come close up to her, they asked her who the king of that country might be, and over what kind of people he ruled; so she directed them to her father's house, but when they got there they found his wife to be a giantess as huge as a mountain, and they were horrified at the sight of her.

"She at once called her husband Antiphates from the place of assembly, and forthwith he set about killing my men. He snatched up one of them, and began to make his dinner off him then and there, whereon the other two ran back to the ships as fast as ever they could. But Antiphates raised a hue-and-cry after them, and thousands of sturdy Laestrygonians sprang up from every quarter—ogres, not men. They threw vast rocks at us from the cliffs as though they had been mere stones, and I heard the horrid sound of the ships crunching up against one another, and the death cries of my men, as the Laestrygonians speared them like fishes and took them home to eat them. While they were thus killing my men within the harbour I drew my sword, cut the cable of my own ship, and told my men to row with all their might if they too would not fare like the rest; so they laid out for their lives, and we were thankful enough when we got into open water out of reach of the rocks they hurled at us. As for the others there was not one of them left.

"Thence we sailed sadly on, glad to have escaped death, though we had lost our comrades, and came to the Aeaean island, where Circe lives—a great and cunning goddess who is own sister to the magician Aeetes—for they are both children of the sun by Perse, who is daughter to Oceanus. We brought our ship into a safe harbour without a word, for some god guided us thither, and having landed we lay there for two days and two nights, worn out in body and mind. When the morning of the third day came I took my spear and my sword, and went away from the ship to reconnoitre, and see if I could discover signs of human handiwork, or hear the sound of voices. Climbing to the top of a high look-out I espied the smoke of Circe's house rising upwards amid a dense forest of trees, and when I saw this I doubted whether, having seen the smoke, I would not go on at once and find out more, but in the end I deemed it best to go back to the ship, give the men their dinners, and send some of them instead of going myself.

"When I had nearly got back to the ship some god took pity upon my solitude, and sent a fine antlered stag right into the middle of my path. He was coming down his pasture in the forest to drink of the river, for the heat of the sun drove him, and as he passed I struck him in the middle of the back; the bronze point of the spear went clean through him, and he lay groaning in the dust until the life went out of him. Then I set my foot upon him, drew my spear from the wound, and laid it down; I also gathered rough grass and rushes and twisted them into a fathom or so of good stout rope, with which I bound the four feet of the noble creature together; having so done I hung him round my neck and walked back to the ship leaning upon my spear, for the stag was much too big for me to be able to carry him on my shoulder, steadying him with one hand. As I threw him down in front of the ship, I called the men and spoke cheeringly man by man to each of them. 'Look here my friends,' said I, 'we are not going to die so much before our time after all, and at any rate we will not starve so long as we have got something to eat and drink on board.' On this they uncovered their heads upon the sea shore and admired the stag, for he was indeed a splendid fellow. Then, when they had feasted their eyes upon him sufficiently, they washed their hands and began to cook him for dinner.

"Thus through the livelong day to the going down of the sun we stayed there eating and drinking our fill, but when the sun went down and it came on dark, we camped upon the sea shore. When the child of morning, rosy-fingered Dawn, appeared, I called a council and said, 'My friends, we are in very great difficulties; listen therefore to me. We have no idea where the sun either sets or rises, so that we do not even know East from West. I see no way out of it; nevertheless, we must try and find one. We are certainly on an island, for I went as high as I could this morning, and saw the sea reaching all round it to the horizon; it lies low, but towards the middle I saw smoke rising from out of a thick forest of trees.'

"Their hearts sank as they heard me, for they remembered how they had been treated by the Laestrygonian Antiphates, and by the savage ogre Polyphemus. They wept bitterly in their dismay, but there was nothing to be got by crying, so I divided them into two companies and set a captain over each; I gave one company to Eurylochus, while I took command of the other myself. Then we cast lots in a helmet, and the lot fell upon Eurylochus; so he set out with his twenty-two men, and they wept, as also did we who were left behind.

"When they reached Circe's house they found it built of cut stones, on a site that could be seen from far, in the middle of the forest. There were wild mountain wolves and lions prowling all round it—poor bewitched creatures whom she had tamed by her enchantments and drugged into subjection. They did not attack my men, but wagged their great tails, fawned upon them, and rubbed their noses lovingly against them. As hounds crowd round their master when they see him coming from dinner—for they know he will bring them something—even so did these wolves and lions with their great claws fawn upon my men, but the men were terribly frightened at seeing such strange creatures. Presently they reached the gates of the goddess's house, and as they stood there they could hear Circe within, singing most beautifully as she worked at her loom, making a web so fine, so soft, and of such dazzling colours as no one but a goddess could weave. On this Polites, whom I valued and trusted more than any other of my men, said, 'There is some one inside working at a loom and singing most beautifully; the whole place resounds with it, let us call her and see whether she is woman or goddess.'

"They called her and she came down, unfastened the door, and bade them enter. They, thinking no evil, followed her, all except Eurylochus, who suspected mischief and staid outside. When she had got them into her house, she set them upon benches and seats and mixed them a mess with cheese, honey, meal, and Pramnian wine, but she drugged it with wicked poisons to make them forget their homes, and when they had drunk she turned them into pigs by a stroke of her wand, and shut them up in her pigsties. They were like pigs—head, hair, and all, and they grunted just as pigs do; but their senses were the same as before, and they remembered everything.

"Thus then were they shut up squealing, and Circe threw them some acorns and beech masts such as pigs eat, but Eurylochus hurried back to tell me about the sad fate of our comrades. He was so overcome with dismay that though he tried to speak he could find no words to do so; his eyes filled with tears and he could only sob and sigh, till at last we forced his story out of him, and he told us what had happened to the others.

"'We went,' said he, 'as you told us, through the forest, and in the middle of it there was a fine house built with cut stones in a place that could be seen from far. There we found a woman, or else she was a goddess, working at her loom and singing sweetly; so the men shouted to her and called her, whereon she at once came down, opened the door, and invited us in. The others did not suspect any mischief so they followed her into the house, but I staid where I was, for I thought there might be some treachery. From that moment I saw them no more, for not one of them ever came out, though I sat a long time watching for them.'

"Then I took my sword of bronze and slung it over my shoulders; I also took my bow, and told Eurylochus to come back with me and show me the way. But he laid hold of me with both his hands and spoke piteously, saying, 'Sir, do not force me to go with you, but let me stay here, for I know you will not bring one of them back with you, nor even return alive yourself; let us rather see if we cannot escape at any rate with the few that are left us, for we may still save our lives.'

"'Stay where you are, then,' answered I, 'eating and drinking at the ship, but I must go, for I am most urgently bound to do so.'

"With this I left the ship and went up inland. When I got through the charmed grove, and was near the great house of the enchantress Circe, I met Mercury with his golden wand, disguised as a young man in the hey-day of his youth and beauty with the down just coming upon his face. He came up to me and took my hand within his own, saying, 'My poor unhappy man, whither are you going over this mountain top, alone and without knowing the way? Your men are shut up in Circe's pigsties, like so many wild boars in their lairs. You surely do not fancy that you can set them free? I can tell you that you will never get back and will have to stay there with the rest of them. But never mind, I will protect you and get you out of your difficulty. Take this herb, which is one of great virtue, and keep it about you when you go to Circe's house, it will be a talisman to you against every kind of mischief.

"'And I will tell you of all the wicked witchcraft that Circe will try to practice upon you. She will mix a mess for you to drink, and she will drug the meal with which she makes it, but she will not be able to charm you, for the virtue of the herb that I shall give you will prevent her spells from working. I will tell you all about it. When Circe strikes you with her wand, draw your sword and spring upon her as though you were going to kill her. She will then be frightened, and will desire you to go to bed with her; on this you must not point blank refuse her, for you want her to set your companions free, and to take good care also of yourself, but you must make her swear solemnly by all the blessed gods that she will plot no further mischief against you, or else when she has got you naked she will unman you and make you fit for nothing.'

"As he spoke he pulled the herb out of the ground and showed me what it was like. The root was black, while the flower was as white as milk; the gods call it Moly, and mortal men cannot uproot it, but the gods can do whatever they like.

"Then Mercury went back to high Olympus passing over the wooded island; but I fared onward to the house of Circe, and my heart was clouded with care as I walked along. When I got to the gates I stood there and called the goddess, and as soon as she heard me she came down, opened the door, and asked me to come in; so I followed her—much troubled in my mind. She set me on a richly decorated seat inlaid with silver, there was a footstool also under my feet, and she mixed a mess in a golden goblet for me to drink; but she drugged it, for she meant me mischief. When she had given it me, and I had drunk it without its charming me, she struck me with her wand. 'There now,' she cried, 'be off to the pigsty, and make your lair with the rest of them.'

"But I rushed at her with my sword drawn as though I would kill her, whereon she fell with a loud scream, clasped my knees, and spoke piteously, saying, 'Who and whence are you? From what place and people have you come? How can it be that my drugs have no power to charm you? Never yet was any man able to stand so much as a taste of the herb I gave you; you must be spell-proof; surely you can be none other than the bold hero Ulysses, who Mercury always said would come here some day with his ship while on his way home from Troy; so be it then; sheathe your sword and let us go to bed, that we may make friends and learn to trust each other.'

"And I answered, 'Circe, how can you expect me to be friendly with you when you have just been turning all my men into pigs? And now that you have got me here myself, you mean me mischief when you ask me to go to bed with you, and will unman me and make me fit for nothing. I shall certainly not consent to go to bed with you unless you will first take your solemn oath to plot no further harm against me.'

"So she swore at once as I had told her, and when she had completed her oath then I went to bed with her.

...[1]

"Thus did she[2] speak and we assented. We stayed with Circe for a whole twelve month feasting upon an untold quantity both of meat and wine. But when the year had passed in the waning of moons and the long days had come round, my men called me apart and said, 'Sir, it is time you began to think about going home, if so be you are to be spared to see your house and native country at all.'

"Thus did they speak and I assented. Thereon through the livelong day to the going down of the sun we feasted our fill on meat and wine, but when the sun went down and it came on dark the men laid themselves down to sleep in the covered cloisters. I, however, after I had got into bed with Circe, besought her by her knees, and the goddess listened to what I had got to say. 'Circe,' said I, 'please to keep the promise you made me about furthering me on my homeward voyage. I want to get back and so do my men, they are always pestering me with their complaints as soon as ever your back is turned.'

"And the goddess answered, 'Ulysses, noble son of Laertes, you shall none of you stay here any longer if you do not want to, but there is another journey which you have got to take before you can sail homewards. You must go to the house of Hades and of dread Proserpine[3] to consult the ghost of the blind Theban prophet Teiresias, whose reason is still unshaken. To him alone has Proserpine left his understanding even in death, but the other ghosts flit about aimlessly.'

"I was dismayed when I heard this. I sat up in bed and wept, and would gladly have lived no longer to see the light of the sun, but presently when I was tired of weeping and tossing myself about, I said, 'And who shall guide me upon this voyage—for the house of Hades is a port that no ship can reach.'

---

1 此处省略基尔克把尤利西斯的同伴变回人形，尤利西斯召唤在海边等候的同伴一起来到基尔克的宫殿的故事。

2 She 指的是基尔克。

3 Proserpine 是冥王 Hades 的妻子。

"'You will want no guide,' she answered; 'raise your mast, set your white sails, sit quite still, and the North Wind will blow you there of itself. When your ship has traversed the waters of Oceanus, you will reach the fertile shore of Proserpine's country with its groves of tall poplars and willows that shed their fruit untimely; here beach your ship upon the shore of Oceanus, and go straight on to the dark abode of Hades. You will find it near the place where the rivers Pyriphlegethon and Cocytus (which is a branch of the river Styx) flow into Acheron[1], and you will see a rock near it, just where the two roaring rivers run into one another.

"'When you have reached this spot, as I now tell you, dig a trench a cubit or so in length, breadth, and depth, and pour into it as a drink-offering to all the dead, first, honey mixed with milk, then wine, and in the third place water—sprinkling white barley meal over the whole. Moreover you must offer many prayers to the poor feeble ghosts, and promise them that when you get back to Ithaca you will sacrifice a barren heifer to them, the best you have, and will load the pyre with good things. More particularly you must promise that Teiresias shall have a black sheep all to himself, the finest in all your flocks.

"'When you shall have thus besought the ghosts with your prayers, offer them a ram and a black ewe, bending their heads towards Erebus[2]; but yourself turn away from them as though you would make towards the river. On this, many dead men's ghosts will come to you, and you must tell your men to skin the two sheep that you have just killed, and offer them as a burnt sacrifice with prayers to Hades and to Proserpine. Then draw your sword and sit there, so as to prevent any other poor ghost from coming near the spilt blood before Teiresias shall have answered your questions. The seer will presently come to you, and will tell you about your voyage—what stages you are to make, and how you are to sail the sea so as to reach your home.'

...

(From Book X)

1　Acheron 是冥界的一条河。

2　Erebus 指的是冥府的一部分。

思考题

QUESTIONS

1 What is the custom of marriage in the Homeric world seen from the book?

2 What lies in common between Laestrygonians and Cyclopes?

3 What are the differences between Laestrygonians and Cyclopes?

4 What is Aeolus' interpretation for Ulysses' coming back to him? What does it tell us about Greeks' understanding of human behavior?

5 Both Circe and Calypso are goddesses. Are there any similarities between them when they first appear in the epic?

6 Why does Ulysses have to go down to Hades before he puts out to sea? Menelaus does something similar before coming back to Sparta. What is that?

7 What is Greeks' imagination of death? How to get into Hades?

8 The poet writes about the food they eat when Circe changes Ulysses' men into swine. There are also descriptions about food in the previous books. Think about the importance of food and tell why it is especially mentioned.

第八章

独探冥府
故旧重逢

导读

INTRODUCTION

　　本章选自《奥德赛》第十一卷。尤利西斯按照基尔克的指导进入冥府，向特瑞西阿斯探问归程，特瑞西阿斯遂将未来之事对英雄一一述说。尤利西斯在冥府见到了众多亲朋故旧的灵魂，包括他的母亲。他离开伊塔卡远征时，母亲尚且健在，不料十多年后再见时却已阴阳殊途。他在特洛伊战场上的战友们的英灵也都来与他对话，阿伽门农讲述了自己回家后如何被妻子和堂兄弟合谋杀害，阿喀琉斯则向他探问父亲和儿子的情况。

　　本卷中尤利西斯所遇之人都是他的亲眷故交，这些人自然不会像蛮族、魔女那样伤害尤利西斯，但他们已经是没有肉体的亡灵。只身漂泊在外，迟迟不能返回故乡的尤利西斯，乍然间在冥府遭遇故旧，这种故土难归、阴阳相隔的复杂况味，诗中虽未言明，读者也应当能够体会，进而理解尤利西斯彼时百感交集的心境。本卷充分展现了古希腊人的生死观和家族观，读者阅读时可多加留意。

选文

SELECTION

"Then, when we had got down to the sea shore we drew our ship into the water and got her mast and sails into her; we also put the sheep on board and took our places, weeping and in great distress of mind. Circe, that great and cunning goddess, sent us a fair wind that blew dead aft and staid steadily with us keeping our sails all the time well filled; so we did whatever wanted doing to the ship's gear and let her go as the wind and helmsman headed her. All day long her sails were full as she held her course over the sea, but when the sun went down and darkness was over all the earth, we got into the deep waters of the river Oceanus, where lie the land and city of the Cimmerians who live enshrouded in mist and darkness which the rays of the sun never pierce neither at his rising nor as he goes down again out of the heavens, but the poor wretches live in one long melancholy night. When we got there we beached the ship, took the sheep out of her, and went along by the waters of Oceanus till we came to the place of which Circe had told us.

"Here Perimedes and Eurylochus held the victims, while I drew my sword and dug the trench a cubit each way. I made a drink-offering to all the dead, first with honey and milk, then with wine, and thirdly with water, and I sprinkled white barley meal over the whole, praying earnestly to the poor feckless ghosts, and promising them that when I got back to Ithaca I would sacrifice a barren heifer for them, the best I had, and would load the pyre with good things. I also particularly promised that Teiresias should have a black sheep to himself, the best in all my flocks. When I had prayed sufficiently to the dead, I cut the throats of the two sheep and let the blood run into the trench, whereon the ghosts came trooping up from Erebus—brides, young bachelors, old men worn out with toil, maids who had been crossed in love, and brave men who had been killed in battle, with their armour still smirched with blood; they came from every quarter and flitted round the trench with a strange kind of screaming sound that made me turn pale with fear. When I saw them coming I told the men to be quick and flay the carcasses of the two dead sheep and make burnt offerings of them, and at the same time to repeat prayers to Hades and to Proserpine; but I sat where I was with my sword drawn and would not let the poor feckless ghosts come near the blood till Teiresias should have answered my questions.

"The first ghost that came was that of my comrade Elpenor[1], for he had not yet been laid beneath the earth. We had left his body unwaked and unburied in Circe's house, for we had had too much else to do. I was very sorry for him, and cried when I saw him: 'Elpenor,' said I, 'how did you come down here into this gloom and darkness? You have got here on foot quicker than I have with my ship.'

"'Sir,' he answered with a groan, 'it was all bad luck, and my own unspeakable drunkenness. I was lying asleep on the top of Circe's house, and never thought of coming down again by the great staircase but fell right off the roof and broke my neck, so my soul came down to the house of Hades. And now I beseech you by all those whom you have left behind you, though they are not here, by your wife, by the father who brought you up when you were a child, and by Telemachus who is the one hope of your house, do what I shall now ask you. I know that when you leave this limbo you will again hold your ship for the Aeaean island. Do not go thence leaving me unwaked and unburied behind you, or I may bring heaven's anger upon you; but burn me with whatever armour I have, build a barrow for me on the sea shore, that may tell people in days to come what a poor unlucky fellow I was, and plant over my grave the oar I used to row with when I was yet alive and with my messmates.' And I said, 'My poor fellow, I will do all that you have asked of me.'

"Thus, then, did we sit and hold sad talk with one another, I on the one side of the trench with my sword held over the blood, and the ghost of my comrade saying all this to me from the other side. Then came the ghost of my dead mother Anticlea, daughter to

---

1 Elpenor 在史诗第十卷中从基尔克的房顶掉下来摔死了。

Autolycus. I had left her alive when I set out for Troy and was moved to tears when I saw her, but even so, for all my sorrow I would not let her come near the blood till I had asked my questions of Teiresias.

"Then came also the ghost of Theban Teiresias, with his golden sceptre in his hand. He knew me and said, 'Ulysses, noble son of Laertes, why, poor man, have you left the light of day and come down to visit the dead in this sad place? Stand back from the trench and withdraw your sword that I may drink of the blood and answer your questions truly.'

"So I drew back, and sheathed my sword, whereon when he had drunk of the blood he began with his prophecy.

"'You want to know,' said he, 'about your return home, but heaven will make this hard for you. I do not think that you will escape the eye of Neptune, who still nurses his bitter grudge against you for having blinded his son. Still, after much suffering you may get home if you can restrain yourself and your companions when your ship reaches the Thrinacian island, where you will find the sheep and cattle belonging to the sun, who sees and gives ear to everything. If you leave these flocks unharmed and think of nothing but of getting home, you may yet after much hardship reach Ithaca; but if you harm them, then I forewarn you of the destruction both of your ship and of your men. Even though you may yourself escape, you will return in bad plight after losing all your men, in another man's ship, and you will find trouble in your house, which will be overrun by high-handed people, who are devouring your substance under the pretext of paying court and making presents to your wife.

"'When you get home you will take your revenge on these suitors; and after you have killed them by force or fraud in your own house, you must take a well made oar and carry it on and on, till you come to a country where the people have never heard of the sea and do not even mix salt with their food, nor do they know anything about ships, and oars that are as the wings of a ship. I will give you this certain token which cannot escape your notice. A wayfarer will meet you and will say it must be a winnowing shovel that you have got upon your shoulder; on this you must fix the oar in the ground and sacrifice a ram, a bull, and a boar to Neptune. Then go home and offer hecatombs to all the gods in heaven one after the other. As for yourself, death shall come to you from the sea, and your life shall ebb away very gently when you are full of years and peace of mind, and your people shall bless you. All that I have said will come true.'

"'This,' I answered, 'must be as it may please heaven, but tell me and tell me and tell me true, I see my poor mother's ghost close by us; she is sitting by the blood without saying a word, and though I am her own son she does not remember me and speak to me; tell me, Sir, how I can make her know me.'

"'That,' said he, 'I can soon do. Any ghost that you let taste of the blood will talk with you like a reasonable being, but if you do not let them have any blood they will go away again.'

"On this the ghost of Teiresias went back to the house of Hades, for his prophecyings had now been spoken, but I sat still where I was until my mother came up and tasted the blood. Then she knew me at once and spoke fondly to me, saying, 'My son, how did you come down to this abode of darkness while you are still alive? It is a hard thing for the living to see these places, for between us and them there are great and terrible waters, and there is Oceanus, which no man can cross on foot, but he must have a good ship to take him. Are you all this time trying to find your way home from Troy, and have you never yet got back to Ithaca nor seen your wife in your own house?'

"'Mother,' said I, 'I was forced to come here to consult the ghost of the Theban prophet Teiresias. I have never yet been near the Achaean land nor set foot on my native country, and I have had nothing but one long series of misfortunes from the very first day that I set out with Agamemnon for Ilius[1], the land of noble steeds, to fight the Trojans. But tell me, and tell me true, in what way did you die? Did you have a long illness, or did heaven vouchsafe you a gentle easy passage to eternity? Tell me also about my father, and the son whom I left behind me, is my property still in their hands, or has some one else got hold of it, who thinks that I shall not return to claim it? Tell me again what my wife intends doing, and in what mind she is; does she live with my son and guard my estate securely, or has she made the best match she could and married again?'

"My mother answered, 'Your wife still remains in your house, but she is in great distress of mind and spends her whole time in tears both night and day. No one as yet has got possession of your fine property, and Telemachus still holds your lands undisturbed. He has to entertain largely, as of course he must, considering his position as a magistrate, and how every one invites him; your father remains at his old place in the country and never

---

1 这是特洛伊的别名。

goes near the town. He has no comfortable bed nor bedding; in the winter he sleeps on the floor in front of the fire with the men and goes about all in rags, but in summer, when the warm weather comes on again, he lies out in the vineyard on a bed of vine leaves thrown any how upon the ground. He grieves continually about your never having come home, and suffers more and more as he grows older. As for my own end it was in this wise: heaven did not take me swiftly and painlessly in my own house, nor was I attacked by any illness such as those that generally wear people out and kill them, but my longing to know what you were doing and the force of my affection for you—this it was that was the death of me.'

"Then I tried to find some way of embracing my poor mother's ghost. Thrice I sprang towards her and tried to clasp her in my arms, but each time she flitted from my embrace as it were a dream or phantom, and being touched to the quick I said to her, 'Mother, why do you not stay still when I would embrace you? If we could throw our arms around one another we might find sad comfort in the sharing of our sorrows even in the house of Hades; does Proserpine want to lay a still further load of grief upon me by mocking me with a phantom only?'

"'My son,' she answered, 'most ill-fated of all mankind, it is not Proserpine that is beguiling you, but all people are like this when they are dead. The sinews no longer hold the flesh and bones together; these perish in the fierceness of consuming fire as soon as life has left the body, and the soul flits away as though it were a dream. Now, however, go back to the light of day as soon as you can, and note all these things that you may tell them to your wife hereafter.'

...[1]

"When Proserpine had dismissed the female ghosts in all directions, the ghost of Agamemnon son of Atreus came sadly up to me, surrounded by those who had perished with him in the house of Aegisthus. As soon as he had tasted the blood, he knew me, and weeping bitterly stretched out his arms towards me to embrace me; but he had no strength nor substance any more, and I too wept and pitied him as I beheld him. 'How did you come by your death,' said I, 'King Agamemnon? Did Neptune raise his winds and waves against you when you were at sea, or did your enemies make an end of you on the main land when you were cattle-lifting or sheep-stealing, or while they were fighting in defence of their

---

1 此处省略一群妇女的灵魂来到尤利西斯身边的内容。

101

wives and city?'

"'Ulysses,' he answered, 'noble son of Laertes, I was not lost at sea in any storm of Neptune's raising, nor did my foes despatch me upon the mainland, but Aegisthus and my wicked wife were the death of me between them. He asked me to his house, feasted me, and then butchered me most miserably as though I were a fat beast in a slaughter house, while all around me my comrades were slain like sheep or pigs for the wedding breakfast, or picnic, or gorgeous banquet of some great nobleman. You must have seen numbers of men killed either in a general engagement, or in single combat, but you never saw anything so truly pitiable as the way in which we fell in that cloister, with the mixing bowl and the loaded tables lying all about, and the ground reeking with our blood. I heard Priam's daughter Cassandra[1] scream as Clytemnestra[2] killed her close beside me. I lay dying upon the earth with the sword in my body, and raised my hands to kill the slut of a murderess, but she slipped away from me; she would not even close my lips nor my eyes when I was dying, for there is nothing in this world so cruel and so shameless as a woman when she has fallen into such guilt as hers was. Fancy murdering her own husband! I thought I was going to be welcomed home by my children and my servants, but her abominable crime has brought disgrace on herself and all women who shall come after—even on the good ones.'

"And I said, 'In truth Jove has hated the house of Atreus[3] from first to last in the matter of their women's counsels. See how many of us fell for Helen's sake, and now it seems that Clytemnestra hatched mischief against you too during your absence.'

"'Be sure, therefore,' continued Agamemnon, 'and not be too friendly even with your own wife. Do not tell her all that you know perfectly well yourself. Tell her a part only, and keep your own counsel about the rest. Not that your wife, Ulysses, is likely to murder you, for Penelope is a very admirable woman, and has an excellent nature. We left her a young bride with an infant at her breast when we set out for Troy. This child no doubt is now grown up happily to man's estate, and he and his father will have a joyful meeting and embrace one another as it is right they should do, whereas my wicked wife did not even allow me the happiness of looking upon my son, but killed me ere I could do so. Furthermore I say—and

---

1 特洛伊战争后，Cassandra 成为阿伽门农的战利品，被带回迈锡尼。

2 Clytemnestra 是阿伽门农的妻子。

3 阿伽门农是 Atreus 的儿子。

lay my saying to your heart—do not tell people when you are bringing your ship to Ithaca, but steal a march upon them, for after all this there is no trusting women. But now tell me, and tell me true, can you give me any news of my son Orestes? Is he in Orchomenus, or at Pylos, or is he at Sparta with Menelaus—for I presume that he is still living.'

"And I said, 'Agamemnon, why do you ask me? I do not know whether your son is alive or dead, and it is not right to talk when one does not know.'

"As we two sat weeping and talking thus sadly with one another the ghost of Achilles came up to us with Patroclus, Antilochus, and Ajax[1] who was the finest and goodliest man of all the Danaans after the son of Peleus[2]. The fleet descendant of Aeacus knew me and spoke piteously, saying, 'Ulysses, noble son of Laertes, what deed of daring will you undertake next, that you venture down to the house of Hades among us silly dead, who are but the ghosts of them that can labour no more?'

"And I said, 'Achilles, son of Peleus, foremost champion of the Achaeans, I came to consult Teiresias, and see if he could advise me about my return home to Ithaca, for I have never yet been able to get near the Achaean land, nor to set foot in my own country, but have been in trouble all the time. As for you, Achilles, no one was ever yet so fortunate as you have been, nor ever will be, for you were adored by all us Argives as long as you were alive, and now that you are here you are a great prince among the dead. Do not, therefore, take it so much to heart even if you are dead.'

"'Say not a word,' he answered, 'in death's favour; I would rather be a paid servant in a poor man's house and be above ground than king of kings among the dead. But give me news about my son; is he gone to the wars and will he be a great soldier, or is this not so? Tell me also if you have heard anything about my father Peleus—does he still rule among the Myrmidons, or do they show him no respect throughout Hellas and Phthia[3] now that he is old and his limbs fail him? Could I but stand by his side, in the light of day, with the same strength that I had when I killed the bravest of our foes upon the plain of Troy—could I but be as I then was and go even for a short time to my father's house, any one who tried to do him violence or supersede him would soon rue it.'

---

1 Patroclus、Antilochus 和 Ajax 都是远征特洛伊的英雄。

2 Peleus 指的是阿喀琉斯。

3 Phthia 是阿喀琉斯统治的城市。

"'I have heard nothing,' I answered, 'of Peleus, but I can tell you all about your son Neoptolemus, for I took him in my own ship from Scyros with the Achaeans. In our councils of war before Troy he was always first to speak, and his judgement was unerring. Nestor and I were the only two who could surpass him; and when it came to fighting on the plain of Troy, he would never remain with the body of his men, but would dash on far in front, foremost of them all in valour. Many a man did he kill in battle—I cannot name every single one of those whom he slew while fighting on the side of the Argives, but will only say how he killed that valiant hero Eurypylus son of Telephus, who was the handsomest man I ever saw except Memnon; many others also of the Ceteians fell around him by reason of a woman's bribes. Moreover, when all the bravest of the Argives went inside the horse that Epeus had made, and it was left to me to settle when we should either open the door of our ambuscade, or close it, though all the other leaders and chief men among the Danaans were drying their eyes and quaking in every limb, I never once saw him turn pale nor wipe a tear from his cheek; he was all the time urging me to break out from the horse—grasping the handle of his sword and his bronze-shod spear, and breathing fury against the foe. Yet when we had sacked the city of Priam he got his handsome share of the prize money and went on board (such is the fortune of war) without a wound upon him, neither from a thrown spear nor in close combat, for the rage of Mars is a matter of great chance.'

"When I had told him this, the ghost of Achilles strode off across a meadow full of asphodel, exulting over what I had said concerning the prowess of his son.

"The ghosts of other dead men stood near me and told me each his own melancholy tale; but that of Ajax son of Telamon alone held aloof—still angry with me for having won the cause in our dispute about the armour of Achilles. Thetis had offered it as a prize, but the Trojan prisoners and Minerva were the judges. Would that I had never gained the day in such a contest, for it cost the life of Ajax, who was foremost of all the Danaans after the son of Peleus, alike in stature and prowess. [1]

"When I saw him I tried to pacify him and said, 'Ajax, will you not forget and forgive even in death, but must the judgement about that hateful armour still rankle with you? It cost us Argives dear enough to lose such a tower of strength as you were to us. We mourned you as much as we mourned Achilles son of Peleus himself, nor can the blame be laid on

---

1　阿喀琉斯死后，众将士争夺他的铠甲，经众人裁判，铠甲最终被尤利西斯获得，埃阿斯羞愤自杀。

anything but on the spite which Jove bore against the Danaans, for it was this that made him counsel your destruction—come hither, therefore, bring your proud spirit into subjection, and hear what I can tell you.'

"He would not answer, but turned away to Erebus and to the other ghosts; nevertheless, I should have made him talk to me in spite of his being so angry, or I should have gone on talking to him, only that there were still others among the dead whom I desired to see."

...

(From Book XI)

思考题

QUESTIONS

1 How do the Greeks deal with the dead body? What is the custom of funeral in Greece?

2 Ulysses goes down to Hades and talks with ghosts. What can we tell about Greeks' view of life and death from their talks?

3 Ulysses twice tries but fails to hug his mother. What would be his feeling then?

4 Do ghosts have reason? What's Ulysses' mother's explanation of the difference between life and death?

5 Achilles is eager to know about his father and son, which shows the hero values much about family. Where else in the book can we see the importance of family?

6 From the first book on, the fate of Agamemnon forms a contrast with Ulysses'. In this book, Agamemnon tells his own story after coming back home. What is the function of his story for the main plot of the epic? What do you expect to read about Ulysses' story?

7 What is Agamemnon's attitude towards women?

8 Ajax does not draw near to Ulysses. Do you think his behavior is accountable?

第九章

塞千歌声
终归故士

導 读

INTRODUCTION

　　本章节选自《奥德赛》第十二卷和第十三卷。在第十二卷中，尤利西斯一行人离开基尔克后又经历了几处险境：尤利西斯独自聆听了塞壬的美妙歌声；他们来到太阳神的岛屿，同伴偷食了太阳神的牛，受到惩罚，葬身海底，只剩下尤利西斯一人逃脱，来到卡吕普索的岛屿。在第十三卷中，费埃克斯人赠送给尤利西斯许多珍贵的礼物，并护送他回到家乡伊塔卡。密涅瓦现身告知尤利西斯家中的境况，并与他一起谋划对策。

　　在《奥德赛》中，充满了各种各样的欺骗，而且大多不被人看作道德上的瑕疵。尤利西斯在他长期的海上冒险中不得不隐瞒身份，否则便可能招来杀身之祸。他能够逃脱独目巨人的毒手，是因为他巧妙地编造了假名；而他在海上遭遇的所有灾难又是起因于他向独目巨人泄露了真名，招致海神的报复。直到尤利西斯回到家乡时，面对自己的保护神密涅瓦，他仍然编造故事，不肯透露真实身份。"掩饰身份——显示身份"，这是《奥德赛》中很多重要故事情节的标准模式。在后文中依然会出现这样的情节，读者阅读时请留意。

选文

SELECTION

...[1]

"Then, being much troubled in mind, I said to my men, 'My friends, it is not right that one or two of us alone should know the prophecies that Circe has made me, I will therefore tell you about them, so that whether we live or die we may do so with our eyes open. First she said we were to keep clear of the Sirens, who sit and sing most beautifully in a field of flowers; but she said I might hear them myself so long as no one else did. Therefore, take me and bind me to the crosspiece half way up the mast; bind me as I stand upright, with a bond so fast that I cannot possibly break away, and lash the rope's ends to the mast itself. If I beg and pray you to set me free, then bind me more tightly still.'

"I had hardly finished telling everything to the men before we reached the island of the two Sirens, for the wind had been very favourable. Then all of a sudden it fell dead calm; there was not a breath of wind nor a ripple upon the water, so the men furled the sails and stowed them; then taking to their oars they whitened the water with the foam they raised in rowing. Meanwhile I look a large wheel of wax and cut it up small with my sword. Then I kneaded the wax in my strong hands till it became soft, which it soon did between the kneading and the rays of the sun-god son of Hyperion. Then I stopped the ears of all my

---

1　此处省略基尔克为尤利西斯预言遭遇险境的内容。

men, and they bound me hands and feet to the mast as I stood upright on the cross piece; but they went on rowing themselves. When we had got within earshot of the land, and the ship was going at a good rate, the Sirens saw that we were getting in shore and began with their singing.

"'Come here,' they sang, 'renowned Ulysses, honour to the Achaean name, and listen to our two voices. No one ever sailed past us without staying to hear the enchanting sweetness of our song—and he who listens will go on his way not only charmed, but wiser, for we know all the ills that the gods laid upon the Argives and Trojans before Troy, and can tell you everything that is going to happen over the whole world.'

"They sang these words most musically, and as I longed to hear them further I made signs by frowning to my men that they should set me free; but they quickened their stroke, and Eurylochus and Perimedes bound me with still stronger bonds till we had got out of hearing of the Sirens' voices. Then my men took the wax from their ears and unbound me."

...[1]

"When we had passed the (Wandering) rocks, with Scylla and terrible Charybdis, we reached the noble island of the sun-god, where were the goodly cattle and sheep belonging to the sun Hyperion. While still at sea in my ship I could bear the cattle lowing as they came home to the yards, and the sheep bleating. Then I remembered what the blind Theban prophet Teiresias had told me, and how carefully Aeaean Circe had warned me to shun the island of the blessed sun-god. So being much troubled I said to the men, 'My men, I know you are hard pressed, but listen while I tell you the prophecy that Teiresias made me, and how carefully Aeaean Circe warned me to shun the island of the blessed sun-god, for it was here, she said, that our worst danger would lie. Head the ship, therefore, away from the island.'

"The men were in despair at this, and Eurylochus at once gave me an insolent answer. 'Ulysses,' said he, 'you are cruel; you are very strong yourself and never get worn out; you seem to be made of iron, and now, though your men are exhausted with toil and want of sleep, you will not let them land and cook themselves a good supper upon this island, but bid them put out to sea and go faring fruitlessly on through the watches of the flying night.

1　此处省略尤利西斯等人经过卡律布狄斯悬崖和怪物斯库拉的内容。

It is by night that the winds blow hardest and do so much damage; how can we escape should one of those sudden squalls spring up from South West or West, which so often wreck a vessel when our lords the gods are unpropitious? Now, therefore, let us obey the behests of night and prepare our supper here hard by the ship; to-morrow morning we will go on board again and put out to sea.'

"Thus spoke Eurylochus, and the men approved his words. I saw that heaven meant us a mischief and said, 'You force me to yield, for you are many against one, but at any rate each one of you must take his solemn oath that if he meet with a herd of cattle or a large flock of sheep, he will not be so mad as to kill a single head of either, but will be satisfied with the food that Circe has given us.'

"They all swore as I bade them, and when they had completed their oath we made the ship fast in a harbour that was near a stream of fresh water, and the men went ashore and cooked their suppers. As soon as they had had enough to eat and drink, they began talking about their poor comrades whom Scylla had snatched up and eaten; this set them weeping and they went on crying till they fell off into a sound sleep.

"In the third watch of the night when the stars had shifted their places, Jove raised a great gale of wind that flew a hurricane so that land and sea were covered with thick clouds, and night sprang forth out of the heavens. When the child of morning, rosy-fingered Dawn, appeared, we brought the ship to land and drew her into a cave wherein the sea-nymphs hold their courts and dances, and I called the men together in council.

"'My friends,' said I, 'we have meat and drink in the ship, let us mind, therefore, and not touch the cattle, or we shall suffer for it; for these cattle and sheep belong to the mighty sun, who sees and gives ear to everything.' And again they promised that they would obey.

"For a whole month the wind blew steadily from the South, and there was no other wind, but only South and East. As long as corn and wine held out the men did not touch the cattle when they were hungry; when, however, they had eaten all there was in the ship, they were forced to go further afield, with hook and line, catching birds, and taking whatever they could lay their hands on; for they were starving. One day, therefore, I went up inland that I might pray heaven to show me some means of getting away. When I had gone far enough to be clear of all my men, and had found a place that was well sheltered from the wind, I washed my hands and prayed to all the gods in Olympus till by and by they sent me off into a sweet sleep.

"Meanwhile Eurylochus had been giving evil counsel to the men, 'Listen to me,' said he, 'my poor comrades. All deaths are bad enough but there is none so bad as famine. Why should not we drive in the best of these cows and offer them in sacrifice to the immortal gods? If we ever get back to Ithaca, we can build a fine temple to the sun-god and enrich it with every kind of ornament; if, however, he is determined to sink our ship out of revenge for these homed cattle, and the other gods are of the same mind, I for one would rather drink salt water once for all and have done with it, than be starved to death by inches in such a desert island as this is.'

"Thus spoke Eurylochus, and the men approved his words. Now the cattle, so fair and goodly, were feeding not far from the ship; the men, therefore, drove in the best of them, and they all stood round them saying their prayers, and using young oak-shoots instead of barley-meal, for there was no barley left. When they had done praying they killed the cows and dressed their carcasses; they cut out the thigh bones, wrapped them round in two layers of fat, and set some pieces of raw meat on top of them. They had no wine with which to make drink-offerings over the sacrifice while it was cooking, so they kept pouring on a little water from time to time while the inward meats were being grilled; then, when the thigh bones were burned and they had tasted the inward meats, they cut the rest up small and put the pieces upon the spits.

"By this time my deep sleep had left me, and I turned back to the ship and to the sea shore. As I drew near I began to smell hot roast meat, so I groaned out a prayer to the immortal gods. 'Father Jove,' I exclaimed, 'and all you other gods who live in everlasting bliss, you have done me a cruel mischief by the sleep into which you have sent me; see what fine work these men of mine have been making in my absence.'

"Meanwhile Lampetie went straight off to the sun and told him we had been killing his cows, whereon he flew into a great rage, and said to the immortals, 'Father Jove, and all you other gods who live in everlasting bliss, I must have vengeance on the crew of Ulysses' ship: they have had the insolence to kill my cows, which were the one thing I loved to look upon, whether I was going up heaven or down again. If they do not square accounts with me about my cows, I will go down to Hades and shine there among the dead.'

"'Sun,' said Jove, 'go on shining upon us gods and upon mankind over the fruitful earth. I will shiver their ship into little pieces with a bolt of white lightning as soon as they get out to sea.'

"I was told all this by Calypso, who said she had heard it from the mouth of Mercury.

"As soon as I got down to my ship and to the sea shore I rebuked each one of the men separately, but we could see no way out of it, for the cows were dead already. And indeed the gods began at once to show signs and wonders among us, for the hides of the cattle crawled about, and the joints upon the spits began to low like cows, and the meat, whether cooked or raw, kept on making a noise just as cows do.

"For six days my men kept driving in the best cows and feasting upon them, but when Jove the son of Saturn had added a seventh day, the fury of the gale abated; we therefore went on board, raised our masts, spread sail, and put out to sea. As soon as we were well away from the island, and could see nothing but sky and sea, the son of Saturn raised a black cloud over our ship, and the sea grew dark beneath it. We did not get on much further, for in another moment we were caught by a terrific squall from the West that snapped the forestays of the mast so that it fell aft, while all the ship's gear tumbled about at the bottom of the vessel. The mast fell upon the head of the helmsman in the ship's stern, so that the bones of his head were crushed to pieces, and he fell overboard as though he were diving, with no more life left in him.

"Then Jove let fly with his thunderbolts, and the ship went round and round, and was filled with fire and brimstone as the lightning struck it. The men all fell into the sea; they were carried about in the water round the ship, looking like so many sea-gulls, but the god presently deprived them of all chance of getting home again."

...[1]

(From Book XII)

Thus did he[2] speak, and they all held their peace throughout the covered cloister, enthralled by the charm of his story, till presently Alcinous began to speak.

---

1 此处省略以下内容：尤利西斯一个人幸存，来到卡吕普索居住的奥古吉埃岛。尤利西斯对费埃克斯人讲完了自己的故事。

2 he 指的是尤利西斯。

"Ulysses," said he, "now that you have reached my house I doubt not you will get home without further misadventure no matter how much you have suffered in the past. To you others, however, who come here night after night to drink my choicest wine and listen to my bard, I would insist as follows. Our guest has already packed up the clothes, wrought gold, and other valuables which you have brought for his acceptance; let us now, therefore, present him further, each one of us, with a large tripod and a cauldron. We will recoup ourselves by the levy of a general rate; for private individuals cannot be expected to bear the burden of such a handsome present."

Every one approved of this, and then they went home to bed each in his own abode. When the child of morning, rosy-fingered Dawn, appeared they hurried down to the ship and brought their cauldrons with them. Alcinous went on board and saw everything so securely stowed under the ship's benches that nothing could break adrift and injure the rowers. Then they went to the house of Alcinous to get dinner, and he sacrificed a bull for them in honour of Jove who is the lord of all. They set the steaks to grill and made an excellent dinner, after which the inspired bard, Demodocus, who was a favourite with every one, sang to them; but Ulysses kept on turning his eyes towards the sun, as though to hasten his setting, for he was longing to be on his way. As one who has been all day ploughing a fallow field with a couple of oxen keeps thinking about his supper and is glad when night comes that he may go and get it, for it is all his legs can do to carry him, even so did Ulysses rejoice when the sun went down, and he at once said to the Phaeacians, addressing himself more particularly to King Alcinous:

"Sir, and all of you, farewell. Make your drink-offerings and send me on my way rejoicing, for you have fulfilled my heart's desire by giving me an escort, and making me presents, which heaven grant that I may turn to good account; may I find my admirable wife living in peace among friends, and may you whom I leave behind me give satisfaction to your wives and children; may heaven vouchsafe you every good grace, and may no evil thing come among your people."

...

As he spoke he crossed the threshold, and Alcinous sent a man to conduct him to his ship and to the sea shore. Arete also sent some maidservants with him—one with a clean shirt and cloak, another to carry his strong box, and a third with corn and wine. When they got to the water side the crew took these things and put them on board, with all the meat and drink; but for Ulysses they spread a rug and a linen sheet on deck that he might sleep soundly in the stern of the ship. Then he too went on board and lay down without a word, but the crew took every man his place and loosed the hawser from the pierced stone to which it had been bound. Thereon, when they began rowing out to sea, Ulysses fell into a deep, sweet, and almost deathlike slumber.

...

When the bright star that heralds the approach of dawn began to show, the ship drew near to land. Now there is in Ithaca a haven of the old merman Phorcys, which lies between two points that break the line of the sea and shut the harbour in. These shelter it from the storms of wind and sea that rage outside, so that, when once within it, a ship may lie without being even moored. At the head of this harbour there is a large olive tree, and at no great distance a fine overarching cavern sacred to the nymphs who are called Naiads. There are mixing bowls within it and wine-jars of stone, and the bees hive there. Moreover, there are great looms of stone on which the nymphs weave their robes of sea purple—very curious to see—and at all times there is water within it. It has two entrances, one facing North by which mortals can go down into the cave, while the other comes from the South and is more mysterious; mortals cannot possibly get in by it, it is the way taken by the gods.

Into this harbour, then, they took their ship, for they knew the place. She had so much way upon her that she ran half her own length on to the shore; when, however, they had landed, the first thing they did was to lift Ulysses with his rug and linen sheet out of the ship, and lay him down upon the sand still fast asleep. Then they took out the presents which Minerva had persuaded the Phaeacians to give him when he was setting out on his voyage homewards. They put these all together by the root of the olive tree, away from the road, for fear some passer by might come and steal them before Ulysses awoke; and then they made the best of their way home again.

But Neptune did not forget the threats with which he had already threatened Ulysses, so he took counsel with Jove. "Father Jove," said he, "I shall no longer be held in any sort of respect among you gods, if mortals like the Phaeacians, who are my own flesh and blood, show such small regard for me. I said I would let Ulysses get home when he had suffered sufficiently. I did not say that he should never get home at all, for I knew you had already nodded your head about it, and promised that he should do so; but now they have brought him in a ship fast asleep and have landed him in Ithaca after loading him with more magnificent presents of bronze, gold, and raiment than he would ever have brought back from Troy, if he had had his share of the spoil and got home without misadventure."

And Jove answered, "What, O Lord of the Earthquake, are you talking about? The gods are by no means wanting in respect for you. It would be monstrous were they to insult one so old and honoured as you are. As regards mortals, however, if any of them is indulging in insolence and treating you disrespectfully, it will always rest with yourself to deal with him as you may think proper, so do just as you please."

"I should have done so at once," replied Neptune, "if I were not anxious to avoid anything that might displease you; now, therefore, I should like to wreck the Phaeacian ship as it is returning from its escort. This will stop them from escorting people in future; and I should also like to bury their city under a huge mountain."

"My good friend," answered Jove, "I should recommend you at the very moment when the people from the city are watching the ship on her way, to turn it into a rock near the land and looking like a ship. This will astonish everybody, and you can then bury their city under the mountain."

When earth-encircling Neptune heard this he went to Scheria where the Phaeacians live, and stayed there till the ship, which was making rapid way, had got close in. Then he went up to it, turned it into stone, and drove it down with the flat of his hand so as to root it in the ground. After this he went away.

The Phaeacians then began talking among themselves, and one would turn towards his neighbour, saying, "Bless my heart, who is it that can have rooted the ship in the sea just as she was getting into port? We could see the whole of her only a moment ago."

This was how they talked, but they knew nothing about it; and Alcinous said, "I remember now the old prophecy of my father. He said that Neptune would be angry with us for taking every one so safely over the sea, and would one day wreck a Phaeacian ship as it was returning from an escort, and bury our city under a high mountain. This was what my old father used to say, and now it is all coming true. Now therefore let us all do as I say; in the first place we must leave off giving people escorts when they come here, and in the next let us sacrifice twelve picked bulls to Neptune that he may have mercy upon us, and not bury our city under the high mountain." When the people heard this they were afraid and got ready the bulls.

Thus did the chiefs and rulers of the Phaeacians pray to king Neptune, standing round his altar; and at the same time Ulysses woke up once more upon his own soil. He had been so long away that he did not know it again; moreover, Jove's daughter Minerva had made it a foggy day, so that people might not know of his having come, and that she might tell him everything without either his wife or his fellow citizens and friends recognising him until he had taken his revenge upon the wicked suitors. Everything, therefore, seemed quite different to him—the long straight tracks, the harbours, the precipices, and the goodly trees, appeared all changed as he started up and looked upon his native land. So he smote his thighs with the flat of his hands and cried aloud despairingly.

"Alas," he exclaimed, "among what manner of people am I fallen? Are they savage and uncivilised or hospitable and humane? Where shall I put all this treasure, and which way shall I go? I wish I had staid over there with the Phaeacians; or I could have gone to some other great chief who would have been good to me and given me an escort. As it is I do not know where to put my treasure, and I cannot leave it here for fear somebody else should get hold of it. In good truth the chiefs and rulers of the Phaeacians have not been dealing fairly by me, and have left me in the wrong country; they said they would take me back to Ithaca and they have not done so: may Jove the protector of suppliants chastise them, for he watches over everybody and punishes those who do wrong. Still, I suppose I must count my goods and see if the crew have gone off with any of them."

He counted his goodly coppers and cauldrons, his gold and all his clothes, but there was nothing missing; still he kept grieving about not being in his own country, and wandered up and down by the shore of the sounding sea bewailing his hard fate. Then Minerva came up to him disguised as a young shepherd of delicate and princely mien, with a good cloak folded double about her shoulders; she had sandals on her comely feet and held a javelin in her hand. Ulysses was glad when he saw her, and went straight up to her.

"My friend," said he, "you are the first person whom I have met with in this country; I salute you, therefore, and beg you to be well disposed towards me. Protect these my goods, and myself too, for I embrace your knees and pray to you as though you were a god. Tell me, then, and tell me truly, what land and country is this? Who are its inhabitants? Am I on an island, or is this the sea board of some continent?"

Minerva answered, "Stranger, you must be very simple, or must have come from somewhere a long way off, not to know what country this is. It is a very celebrated place, and everybody knows it East and West. It is rugged and not a good driving country, but it is by no means a bad island for what there is of it. It grows any quantity of corn and also wine, for it is watered both by rain and dew; it breeds cattle also and goats; all kinds of timber grow here, and there are watering places where the water never runs dry; so, sir, the name of Ithaca is known even as far as Troy, which I understand to be a long way off from this Achaean country."

Ulysses was glad at finding himself, as Minerva told him, in his own country, and he began to answer, but he did not speak the truth, and made up a lying story in the instinctive wiliness of his heart.

"I heard of Ithaca," said he, "when I was in Crete beyond the seas, and now it seems I have reached it with all these treasures. I have left as much more behind me for my children, but am flying because I killed Orsilochus son of Idomeneus, the fleetest runner in Crete. I killed him because he wanted to rob me of the spoils I had got from Troy with so much trouble and danger both on the field of battle and by the waves of the weary sea; he said I had not served his father loyally at Troy as vassal, but had set myself up as an independent ruler, so I lay in wait for him with one of my followers by the road side, and speared him as he was coming into town from the country. It was a very dark night and nobody saw us; it was not known, therefore, that I had killed him, but as soon as I had done so I went to a ship and besought the owners, who were Phoenicians, to take me on board and set me in Pylos or in Elis where the Epeans rule, giving them as much spoil as satisfied them. They meant no guile, but the wind drove them off their course, and we sailed on till we came hither by night. It was all we could do to get inside the harbour, and none of us said a word about supper though we wanted it badly, but we all went on shore and lay down just as we were. I was very tired and fell asleep directly, so they took my goods out of the ship, and placed them beside me where I was lying upon the sand. Then they sailed away to Sidonia, and I was left here in great distress of mind."

Such was his story, but Minerva smiled and caressed him with her hand. Then she took the form of a woman, fair, stately, and wise, "He must be indeed a shifty lying fellow," said she, "who could surpass you in all manner of craft even though you had a god for your antagonist. Dare devil that you are, full of guile, unwearying in deceit, can you not drop your tricks and your instinctive falsehood, even now that you are in your own country again? We will say no more, however, about this, for we can both of us deceive upon occasion—you are the most accomplished counsellor and orator among all mankind, while I for diplomacy and subtlety have no equal among the gods. Did you not know Jove's daughter Minerva—me, who have been ever with you, who kept watch over you in all your troubles, and who made the Phaeacians take so great a liking to you? And now, again, I am come here to talk things over with you, and help you to hide the treasure I made the Phaeacians give you; I want to tell you about the troubles that await you in your own house; you have got to face them, but tell no one, neither man nor woman, that you have come home again. Bear everything, and put up with every man's insolence, without a word."

...

As she spoke the goddess dispersed the mist and the land appeared. Then Ulysses rejoiced at finding himself again in his own land, and kissed the bounteous soil; he lifted up his hands and prayed to the nymphs, saying, "Naiad nymphs, daughters of Jove, I made sure that I was never again to see you, now therefore I greet you with all loving salutations, and I will bring you offerings as in the old days, if Jove's redoubtable daughter will grant me life, and bring my son to manhood."

"Take heart, and do not trouble yourself about that," rejoined Minerva, "let us rather set about stowing your things at once in the cave, where they will be quite safe. Let us see how we can best manage it all."

Therewith she went down into the cave to look for the safest hiding places, while Ulysses brought up all the treasure of gold, bronze, and good clothing which the Phaeacians had given him. They stowed everything carefully away, and Minerva set a stone against the door of the cave. Then the two sat down by the root of the great olive, and consulted how to compass the destruction of the wicked suitors.

"Ulysses," said Minerva, "noble son of Laertes, think how you can lay hands on these disreputable people who have been lording it in your house these three years, courting your wife and making wedding presents to her, while she does nothing but lament your absence, giving hope and sending encouraging messages to every one of them, but meaning the very opposite of all she says."

(From Book XIII)

思考题

QUESTIONS

1 What are the Sirens singing about? Is it the reason why Ulysses is attracted?

2 Why does Ulysses insist on listening to the Sirens' song? What can we tell about his character?

3 What do the people offer to gods when they pray?

4 Why do Ulysses' men eat Sun's cows in spite of Circe's warning? Why doesn't Ulysses eat?

5 Book XIII mentions several times the presents given to Ulysses by the Phaeacians. What are the presents? What is Ulysses' attitude towards receiving the presents?

6 What is the fate of the Phaeacians after they escort Ulysses? What is the relation between men and gods in general?

7 Why does Ulysses lie to Minerva? What can we tell about his character?

8 The Phaeacians take the sleeping Ulysses down from the ship and lay him on the ground. Then they go back home without rousing him up. In *Poetics* Aristotle uses the plot to illustrate the concept of "improbability", i.e. "unconvincing possibility". What is your comment on the plot? Do you think it is improbable?

第十章

良人难认 保姆识主

导读

本章选自《奥德赛》第十八卷和第十九卷。本书在节选时跳过了第十四卷到第十七卷，这四卷主要讲述的是尤利西斯在进城之前先到田庄暗访牧猪奴，特勒马科斯回到伊塔卡，父子二人在田庄相认，共同商议如何对付求婚人，尤利西斯化装成异乡人来到自己家中求乞。在第十八卷中，佩涅洛佩用缓兵之计向求婚者索要结婚礼物。第十九卷里，佩涅洛佩和化装为异乡人的尤利西斯见面交谈，佩涅洛佩没有认出自己的丈夫。尤利西斯的保姆在为他洗脚时，认出了他腿上的伤疤，尤利西斯让她不要声张，以免泄露身份。

本章追忆了尤利西斯小时候在外公家打猎时被野猪刺伤的情节，将时间拉回到几十年前，为塑造更丰富、更立体的尤利西斯形象提供了一个时空上的纵深。这部史诗所崇尚的家庭价值往往通过家族成员间的亲切交往而展现，这也使得尤利西斯此时的处境更显悲凉：明明在自己的家园，却被迫假扮成异乡人；最爱的妻子近在咫尺，却不能相认。

选文

SELECTION

...

Then Minerva put it into the mind of Penelope to show herself to the suitors, that she might make them still more enamoured of her, and win still further honour from her son and husband. So she feigned a mocking laugh and said, "Eurynome[1], I have changed my mind, and have a fancy to show myself to the suitors although I detest them. I should like also to give my son a hint that he had better not have anything more to do with them. They speak fairly enough but they mean mischief."

"My dear child," answered Eurynome, "all that you have said is true, go and tell your son about it, but first wash yourself and anoint your face. Do not go about with your cheeks all covered with tears; it is not right that you should grieve so incessantly; for Telemachus, whom you always prayed that you might live to see with a beard, is already grown up."

"I know, Eurynome," replied Penelope, "that you mean well, but do not try and persuade me to wash and to anoint myself, for heaven robbed me of all my beauty on the day my husband sailed; nevertheless, tell Autonoe and Hippodamia[2] that I want them. They must be with me when I am in the cloister; I am not going among the men alone; it would

---

1　Eurynome 是家里的女管家。

2　Autonoe 和 Hippodamia 是两名女仆。

not be proper for me to do so."

On this the old woman went out of the room to bid the maids go to their mistress. In the meantime Minerva bethought her of another matter, and sent Penelope off into a sweet slumber; so she lay down on her couch and her limbs became heavy with sleep. Then the goddess shed grace and beauty over her that all the Achaeans might admire her. She washed her face with the ambrosial loveliness that Venus wears when she goes dancing with the Graces; she made her taller and of a more commanding figure, while as for her complexion it was whiter than sawn ivory. When Minerva had done all this she went away, whereon the maids came in from the women's room and woke Penelope with the sound of their talking.

"What an exquisitely delicious sleep I have been having," said she, as she passed her hands over her face, "in spite of all my misery. I wish Diana would let me die so sweetly now at this very moment, that I might no longer waste in despair for the loss of my dear husband, who possessed every kind of good quality and was the most distinguished man among the Achaeans."

With these words she came down from her upper room, not alone but attended by two of her maidens, and when she reached the suitors she stood by one of the bearing-posts supporting the roof of the cloister, holding a veil before her face, and with a staid maid servant on either side of her. As they beheld her the suitors were so overpowered and became so desperately enamoured of her, that each one prayed he might win her for his own bed fellow.

"Telemachus," said she, addressing her son, "I fear you are no longer so discreet and well conducted as you used to be. When you were younger you had a greater sense of propriety; now, however, that you are grown up, though a stranger to look at you would take you for the son of a well to do father as far as size and good looks go, your conduct is by no means what it should be. What is all this disturbance that has been going on, and how came you to allow a stranger[1] to be so disgracefully ill-treated? What would have happened if he had suffered serious injury while a suppliant in our house? Surely this would have been very discreditable to you."

"I am not surprised, my dear mother, at your displeasure," replied Telemachus, "I

1　尤利西斯化装成异乡人来到自己家中求乞。

understand all about it and know when things are not as they should be, which I could not do when I was younger; I cannot, however, behave with perfect propriety at all times. First one and then another of these wicked people here keeps driving me out of my mind, and I have no one to stand by me. After all, however, this fight between Irus[1] and the stranger did not turn out as the suitors meant it to do, for the stranger got the best of it. I wish Father Jove, Minerva, and Apollo would break the neck of every one of these wooers of yours, some inside the house and some out; and I wish they might all be as limp as Irus is over yonder in the gate of the outer court. See how he nods his head like a drunken man; he has had such a thrashing that he cannot stand on his feet nor get back to his home, wherever that may be, for he has no strength left in him."

Thus did they converse. Eurymachus[2] then came up and said, "Queen Penelope, daughter of Icarius, if all the Achaeans in Iasian Argos could see you at this moment, you would have still more suitors in your house by tomorrow morning, for you are the most admirable woman in the whole world both as regards personal beauty and strength of understanding."

To this Penelope replied, "Eurymachus, heaven robbed me of all my beauty whether of face or figure when the Argives set sail for Troy and my dear husband with them. If he were to return and look after my affairs, I should both be more respected and show a better presence to the world. As it is, I am oppressed with care, and with the afflictions which heaven has seen fit to heap upon me. My husband foresaw it all, and when he was leaving home he took my right wrist in his hand—'Wife,' he said, 'we shall not all of us come safe home from Troy, for the Trojans fight well both with bow and spear. They are excellent also at fighting from chariots, and nothing decides the issue of a fight sooner than this. I know not, therefore, whether heaven will send me back to you, or whether I may not fall over there at Troy. In the meantime do you look after things here. Take care of my father and mother as at present, and even more so during my absence, but when you see our son growing a beard, then marry whom you will, and leave this your present home.' This is what he said and now it is all coming true. A night will come when I shall have to yield myself to a marriage which I detest, for Jove has taken from me all hope of happiness. This further grief, moreover, cuts me to the very heart. You suitors are not wooing me after the custom of my country. When

---

1 Irus 是乞丐的名字。尤利西斯与他比武并战胜了他。

2 Eurymachus 是一个求婚者。

men are courting a woman who they think will be a good wife to them and who is of noble birth, and when they are each trying to win her for himself, they usually bring oxen and sheep to feast the friends of the lady, and they make her magnificent presents, instead of eating up other people's property without paying for it."

This was what she said, and Ulysses was glad when he heard her trying to get presents out of the suitors, and flattering them with fair words which he knew she did not mean.

Then Antinous[1] said, "Queen Penelope, daughter of Icarius, take as many presents as you please from any one who will give them to you; it is not well to refuse a present; but we will not go about our business nor stir from where we are, till you have married the best man among us whoever he may be."

The others applauded what Antinous had said, and each one sent his servant to bring his present. Antinous's man returned with a large and lovely dress most exquisitely embroidered. It had twelve beautifully made brooch pins of pure gold with which to fasten it. Eurymachus immediately brought her a magnificent chain of gold and amber beads that gleamed like sunlight. Eurydamas's two men returned with some earrings fashioned into three brilliant pendants which glistened most beautifully; while king Pisander son of Polyctor gave her a necklace of the rarest workmanship, and every one else brought her a beautiful present of some kind.

...

(From Book XVIII)

...[2]

Then she[3] said to her head waiting woman Eurynome, "Bring a seat with a fleece upon it, for the stranger to sit upon while he tells his story, and listens to what I have to say. I wish to ask him some questions."

Eurynome brought the seat at once and set a fleece upon it, and as soon as Ulysses had

---

1　Antinous 是一个求婚者。

2　此处省略尤利西斯和特勒马科斯将厅堂里的武器藏起来的内容。

3　She 指的是佩涅洛佩（Penelope）。

sat down Penelope began by saying, "Stranger, I shall first ask you who and whence are you? Tell me of your town and parents."

"Madam," answered Ulysses, "who on the face of the whole earth can dare to chide with you? Your fame reaches the firmament of heaven itself; you are like some blameless king, who upholds righteousness, as the monarch over a great and valiant nation: the earth yields its wheat and barley, the trees are loaded with fruit, the ewes bring forth lambs, and the sea abounds with fish by reason of his virtues, and his people do good deeds under him. Nevertheless, as I sit here in your house, ask me some other question and do not seek to know my race and family, or you will recall memories that will yet more increase my sorrow. I am full of heaviness, but I ought not to sit weeping and wailing in another person's house, nor is it well to be thus grieving continually. I shall have one of the servants or even yourself complaining of me, and saying that my eyes swim with tears because I am heavy with wine."

Then Penelope answered, "Stranger, heaven robbed me of all beauty, whether of face or figure, when the Argives set sail for Troy and my dear husband with them. If he were to return and look after my affairs I should be both more respected and should show a better presence to the world. As it is, I am oppressed with care, and with the afflictions which heaven has seen fit to heap upon me. The chiefs from all our islands—Dulichium, Same, and Zacynthus, as also from Ithaca itself, are wooing me against my will and are wasting my estate. I can therefore show no attention to strangers, nor suppliants, nor to people who say that they are skilled artisans, but am all the time broken-hearted about Ulysses. They want me to marry again at once, and I have to invent stratagems in order to deceive them. In the first place heaven put it in my mind to set up a great tambour-frame in my room, and to begin working upon an enormous piece of fine needlework. Then I said to them, 'Sweethearts, Ulysses is indeed dead, still, do not press me to marry again immediately; wait—for I would not have my skill in needlework perish unrecorded—till I have finished making a pall for the hero Laertes, to be ready against the time when death shall take him. He is very rich, and the women of the place will talk if he is laid out without a pall.' This was what I said, and they assented; whereon I used to keep working at my great web all day long, but at night I would unpick the stitches again by torch light. I fooled them in this way for three years without their finding it out, but as time wore on and I was now in my fourth year, in the waning of moons, and many days had been accomplished, those good for nothing hussies

127

my maids betrayed me to the suitors, who broke in upon me and caught me; they were very angry with me, so I was forced to finish my work whether I would or no. And now I do not see how I can find any further shift for getting out of this marriage. My parents are putting great pressure upon me, and my son chafes at the ravages the suitors are making upon his estate, for he is now old enough to understand all about it and is perfectly able to look after his own affairs, for heaven has blessed him with an excellent disposition. Still, notwithstanding all this, tell me who you are and where you come from—for you must have had father and mother of some sort; you cannot be the son of an oak or of a rock."

...[1]

Many a plausible tale did Ulysses further tell her, and Penelope wept as she listened, for her heart was melted. As the snow wastes upon the mountain tops when the winds from South East and West have breathed upon it and thawed it till the rivers run bank full with water, even so did her cheeks overflow with tears for the husband who was all the time sitting by her side. Ulysses felt for her and was sorry for her, but he kept his eyes as hard as horn or iron without letting them so much as quiver, so cunningly did he restrain his tears. Then, when she had relieved herself by weeping, she turned to him again and said: "Now, stranger, I shall put you to the test and see whether or no you really did entertain my husband and his men, as you say you did. Tell me, then, how he was dressed, what kind of a man he was to look at, and so also with his companions."

"Madam," answered Ulysses, "it is such a long time ago that I can hardly say. Twenty years are come and gone since he left my home, and went elsewhither; but I will tell you as well as I can recollect. Ulysses wore a mantle of purple wool, double lined, and it was fastened by a gold brooch with two catches for the pin. On the face of this there was a device that showed a dog holding a spotted fawn between his fore paws, and watching it as it lay panting upon the ground. Every one marveled at the way in which these things had been done in gold, the dog looking at the fawn, and strangling it, while the fawn was struggling convulsively to escape. As for the shirt that he wore next his skin, it was so soft that it fitted him like the skin of an onion, and glistened in the sunlight to the admiration of all the women who beheld it. Furthermore I say, and lay my saying to your heart, that

---

1　此处省略陌生人（尤利西斯）编造的故事，他自称来自克里特岛，尤利西斯远征特洛伊途中曾到访克里特，并受其招待。

I do not know whether Ulysses wore these clothes when he left home, or whether one of his companions had given them to him while he was on his voyage; or possibly some one at whose house he was staying made him a present of them, for he was a man of many friends and had few equals among the Achaeans. I myself gave him a sword of bronze and a beautiful purple mantle, double lined, with a shirt that went down to his feet, and I sent him on board his ship with every mark of honour. He had a servant with him, a little older than himself, and I can tell you what he was like; his shoulders were hunched, he was dark, and he had thick curly hair. His name was Eurybates, and Ulysses treated him with greater familiarity than he did any of the others, as being the most like-minded with himself."

Penelope was moved still more deeply as she heard the indisputable proofs that Ulysses laid before her; and when she had again found relief in tears she said to him, "Stranger, I was already disposed to pity you, but henceforth you shall be honoured and made welcome in my house. It was I who gave Ulysses the clothes you speak of. I took them out of the store room and folded them up myself, and I gave him also the gold brooch to wear as an ornament. Alas! I shall never welcome him home again. It was by an ill fate that he ever set out for that detested city whose very name I cannot bring myself even to mention."

...[1]

To this Penelope said, "My dear sir, of all the guests who ever yet came to my house there never was one who spoke in all things with such admirable propriety as you do. There happens to be in the house a most respectable old woman—the same who received my poor dear husband in her arms the night he was born, and nursed him in infancy. She is very feeble now, but she shall wash your feet." "Come here," said she, "Euryclea, and wash your master's age-mate; I suppose Ulysses' hands and feet are very much the same now as his are, for trouble ages all of us dreadfully fast."

On these words the old woman covered her face with her hands; she began to weep and made lamentation saying, "My dear child, I cannot think whatever I am to do with you. I am certain no one was ever more god-fearing than yourself, and yet Jove hates you. No one in the whole world ever burned him more thigh bones, nor gave him finer hecatombs when you prayed you might come to a green old age yourself and see your son grow up to take after you: yet see how he has prevented you alone from ever getting back to your own home.

---

1 此处省略异乡人安慰佩涅洛佩说尤利西斯一定会回家的情景。

I have no doubt the women in some foreign palace which Ulysses has got to are gibing at him as all these sluts here have been gibing at you. I do not wonder at your not choosing to let them wash you after the manner in which they have insulted you; I will wash your feet myself gladly enough, as Penelope has said that I am to do so; I will wash them both for Penelope's sake and for your own, for you have raised the most lively feelings of compassion in my mind; and let me say this moreover, which pray attend to; we have had all kinds of strangers in distress come here before now, but I make bold to say that no one ever yet came who was so like Ulysses in figure, voice, and feet as you are."

"Those who have seen us both," answered Ulysses, "have always said we were wonderfully like each other, and now you have noticed it too."

Then the old woman took the cauldron in which she was going to wash his feet, and poured plenty of cold water into it, adding hot till the bath was warm enough. Ulysses sat by the fire, but ere long he turned away from the light, for it occurred to him that when the old woman had hold of his leg she would recognise a certain scar which it bore, whereon the whole truth would come out. And indeed as soon as she began washing her master, she at once knew the scar as one that had been given him by a wild boar when he was hunting on Mt. Parnassus with his excellent grandfather Autolycus—who was the most accomplished thief and perjurer in the whole world—and with the sons of Autolycus. Mercury himself had endowed him with this gift, for he used to burn the thigh bones of goats and kids to him, so he took pleasure in his companionship. It happened once that Autolycus had gone to Ithaca and had found the child of his daughter just born. As soon as he had done supper Euryclea set the infant upon his knees and said, "Autolycus, you must find a name for your grandson; you greatly wished that you might have one."

"Son-in-law and daughter," replied Autolycus, "call the child thus: I am highly displeased with a large number of people in one place and another, both men and women; so name the child 'Ulysses,' or the child of anger. When he grows up and comes to visit his mother's family on Mt. Parnassus, where my possessions lie, I will make him a present and will send him on his way rejoicing."

Ulysses, therefore, went to Parnassus to get the presents from Autolycus, who with his sons shook hands with him and gave him welcome. His grandmother Amphithea threw her arms about him, and kissed his head, and both his beautiful eyes, while Autolycus desired his sons to get dinner ready, and they did as he told them. They brought in a five year old bull, flayed it, made it ready and divided it into joints; these they then cut carefully up into smaller pieces and spitted them; they roasted them sufficiently and served the portions round. Thus through the livelong day to the going down of the sun they feasted, and every man had his full share so that all were satisfied; but when the sun set and it came on dark, they went to bed and enjoyed the boon of sleep.

When the child of morning, rosy-fingered Dawn, appeared, the sons of Autolycus went out with their hounds hunting, and Ulysses went too. They climbed the wooded slopes of Parnassus and soon reached its breezy upland valleys; but as the sun was beginning to beat upon the fields, fresh-risen from the slow still currents of Oceanus, they came to a mountain dell. The dogs were in front searching for the tracks of the beast they were chasing, and after them came the sons of Autolycus, among whom was Ulysses, close behind the dogs, and he had a long spear in his hand. Here was the lair of a huge boar among some thick brushwood, so dense that the wind and rain could not get through it, nor could the sun's rays pierce it, and the ground underneath lay thick with fallen leaves. The boar heard the noise of the men's feet, and the hounds baying on every side as the huntsmen came up to him, so he rushed from his lair, raised the bristles on his neck, and stood at bay with fire flashing from his eyes. Ulysses was the first to raise his spear and try to drive it into the brute, but the boar was too quick for him, and charged him sideways, ripping him above the knee with a gash that tore deep though it did not reach the bone. As for the boar, Ulysses hit him on the right shoulder, and the point of the spear went right through him, so that he fell groaning in the dust until the life went out of him. The sons of Autolycus busied themselves with the carcass of the boar, and bound Ulysses' wound; then, after saying a spell to stop the bleeding, they went home as fast as they could. But when Autolycus and his sons had thoroughly healed Ulysses, they made him some splendid presents, and sent him back to Ithaca with much mutual good will. When he got back, his father and mother were rejoiced to see him, and asked him all about it, and how he had hurt himself to get the scar; so he told them how the boar had ripped him when he was out hunting with Autolycus and his sons on Mt. Parnassus.

As soon as Euryclea had got the scarred limb in her hands and had well hold of it, she recognised it and dropped the foot at once. The leg fell into the bath, which rang out and was overturned, so that all the water was spilt on the ground; Euryclea's eyes between her joy and her grief filled with tears, and she could not speak, but she caught Ulysses by the beard and said, "My dear child, I am sure you must be Ulysses himself, only I did not know you till I had actually touched and handled you."

As she spoke she looked towards Penelope, as though wanting to tell her that her dear husband was in the house, but Penelope was unable to look in that direction and observe what was going on, for Minerva had diverted her attention; so Ulysses caught Euryclea by the throat with his right hand and with his left drew her close to him, and said, "Nurse, do you wish to be the ruin of me, you who nursed me at your own breast, now that after twenty years of wandering I am at last come to my own home again? Since it has been borne in upon you by heaven to recognise me, hold your tongue, and do not say a word about it to any one else in the house, for if you do I tell you—and it shall surely be—that if heaven grants me to take the lives of these suitors, I will not spare you, though you are my own nurse, when I am killing the other women."

"My child," answered Euryclea, "what are you talking about? You know very well that nothing can either bend or break me. I will hold my tongue like a stone or a piece of iron; furthermore let me say, and lay my saying to your heart, when heaven has delivered the suitors into your hand, I will give you a list of the women in the house who have been ill-behaved, and of those who are guiltless."

...

(From Book XIX)

思考题

QUESTIONS

1　When Penelope appears before the suitors, she first speaks to Telemachus. Tell from her words what a man of good breeding should look like, and in what way he should behave.

2　What is the right way to treat a suppliant according to the Greek custom?

3　What are the presents the suitors give Penelope? Ulysses is happy to see Penelope ask suitors for presents. What conclusion can we draw from this about their values?

4　When a person's name appears, it is usually followed by "son of someone", like "king Pisander son of Polyctor". This is the convention in the epic. Can you find other examples in previous chapters? What can you tell about Greek society by this turn of speech?

5　Does Penelope tell truth when she says Ulysses allows her to marry another man?

6　The epic is full of frauds and tricks. Try to find out what is not true in Ulysses' and Penelope's words.

7　People often have to recognize one another by tokens in Greek mythology. What is the token by which Ulysses' nurse recognizes him?

8　A story is told in the chapter in which Ulysses goes for hunting in his grandfather's home as a boy. How is the story related to Ulysses the hero? How is it related to the theme of the epic?

第十一章

神力穿杨
尽诛强敌

导 读

本章选自《奥德赛》第二十一卷和第二十二卷。在第二十一卷中，面对众多求婚者，佩涅洛佩心生一计，她拿出尤利西斯用过的强弓，宣布凡能拉动强弓并能一箭射穿十二个斧孔的人，便能娶她为妻。众多求婚者都不能拉动强弓，只有化装成乞丐的尤利西斯拉开了强弓，一箭就射穿了十二个斧孔。在第二十二卷中，尤利西斯与特勒马科斯将长年耗费自家财产的众多求婚人困在厅堂内，诛杀殆尽，报仇雪恨。

在古希腊人的观念里，在宴会上惨遭杀戮是非常悲惨的，因为美好的现世享乐与可怕的死亡形成了鲜明的对比。阿伽门农就是这样被妻子和她的情人杀害的，而他的命运在史诗中一直是尤利西斯的衬托。如今尤利西斯没有像他的老战友那样暗淡收场，而是利用自己的聪明才智，运筹帷幄，绝地反击，杀尽求婚人，取得完胜。至此二人的命运对比也终于完成。佩涅洛佩应对求婚人的方式与尤利西斯截然不同，她采用了以柔克刚、长期拖延的策略，终于等到丈夫归来。他们的儿子特勒马科斯在本章中也表现得非常成熟，主持大局英勇果断，对求婚人的这场大杀戮成为他的成年礼。

选文

SELECTION

...

Penelope presently reached the oak threshold of the store-room; the carpenter had planned this duly, and had drawn a line on it so as to get it quite straight; he had then set the door posts into it and hung the doors. She loosed the strap from the handle of the door, put in the key, and drove it straight home to shoot back the bolts that held the doors; these flew open with a noise like a bull bellowing in a meadow, and Penelope stepped upon the raised platform, where the chests stood in which the fair linen and clothes were laid by along with fragrant herbs: reaching thence, she took down the bow with its bow case from the peg on which it hung. She sat down with it on her knees, weeping bitterly as she took the bow out of its case, and when her tears had relieved her, she went to the cloister where the suitors were, carrying the bow and the quiver, with the many deadly arrows that were inside it. Along with her came her maidens, bearing a chest that contained much iron and bronze which her husband had won as prizes. When she reached the suitors, she stood by one of the bearing-posts supporting the roof of the cloister, holding a veil before her face, and with a maid on either side of her. Then she said:

"Listen to me you suitors, who persist in abusing the hospitality of this house because its owner has been long absent, and without other pretext than that you want to marry me; this, then, being the prize that you are contending for, I will bring out the mighty bow of

Ulysses, and whomsoever of you shall string it most easily and send his arrow through each one of twelve axes, him will I follow and quit this house of my lawful husband, so goodly, and so abounding in wealth. But even so I doubt not that I shall remember it in my dreams."

...[1]

...Then, when they had made their offerings and had drunk each as much as he desired, Ulysses craftily said:

"Suitors of the illustrious queen, listen that I may speak even as I am minded. I appeal more especially to Eurymachus, and to Antinous who has just spoken with so much reason. Cease shooting for the present and leave the matter to the gods, but in the morning let heaven give victory to whom it will. For the moment, however, give me the bow that I may prove the power of my hands among you all, and see whether I still have as much strength as I used to have, or whether travel and neglect have made an end of it."

This made them all very angry, for they feared he might string the bow, Antinous therefore rebuked him fiercely saying, "Wretched creature, you have not so much as a grain of sense in your whole body; you ought to think yourself lucky in being allowed to dine unharmed among your betters, without having any smaller portion served you than we others have had, and in being allowed to hear our conversation. No other beggar or stranger has been allowed to hear what we say among ourselves; the wine must have been doing you a mischief, as it does with all those who drink immoderately. It was wine that inflamed the Centaur Eurytion when he was staying with Peirithous[2] among the Lapithae[3]. When the wine had got into his head, he went mad and did ill deeds about the house of Peirithous; this angered the heroes who were there assembled, so they rushed at him and cut off his ears and nostrils; then they dragged him through the doorway out of the house, so he went away crazed, and bore the burden of his crime, bereft of understanding. Henceforth, therefore, there was war between mankind and the centaurs, but he brought it upon himself through his own drunkenness. In like manner I can tell you that it will go hardly with you if you string the bow: you will find no mercy from any one here, for we shall at once ship you off

---

1 此处省略求婚人尝试拉弓射箭但未能成功的情景。

2 Peirithous 是拉皮泰人（Lapithae）的国王，他的婚礼上邀请了马人（Centaurs）参加，但马人却企图抢劫新娘和其他女宾，国王庇里托俄斯率众与马人作战，夺回被抢走的妇女。

3 Lapithae 是拉皮泰人，居住在塞萨利（Thessaly）境内。

to king Echetus, who kills every one that comes near him: you will never get away alive, so drink and keep quiet without getting into a quarrel with men younger than yourself."

Penelope then spoke to him. "Antinous," said she, "it is not right that you should ill-treat any guest of Telemachus who comes to this house. If the stranger should prove strong enough to string the mighty bow of Ulysses, can you suppose that he would take me home with him and make me his wife? Even the man himself can have no such idea in his mind: none of you need let that disturb his feasting; it would be out of all reason."

"Queen Penelope," answered Eurymachus, "we do not suppose that this man will take you away with him; it is impossible; but we are afraid lest some of the baser sort, men or women among the Achaeans, should go gossiping about and say, 'These suitors are a feeble folk; they are paying court to the wife of a brave man whose bow not one of them was able to string, and yet a beggarly tramp who came to the house strung it at once and sent an arrow through the iron.' This is what will be said, and it will be a scandal against us."

"Eurymachus," Penelope answered, "people who persist in eating up the estate of a great chieftain and dishonouring his house must not expect others to think well of them. Why then should you mind if men talk as you think they will? This stranger is strong and well-built, he says moreover that he is of noble birth. Give him the bow, and let us see whether he can string it or no. I say—and it shall surely be—that if Apollo vouchsafes him the glory of stringing it, I will give him a cloak and shirt of good wear, with a javelin to keep off dogs and robbers, and a sharp sword. I will also give him sandals, and will see him sent safely wherever he wants to go."

Then Telemachus said, "Mother, I am the only man either in Ithaca or in the islands that are over against Elis[1] who has the right to let any one have the bow or to refuse it. No one shall force me one way or the other, not even though I choose to make the stranger a present of the bow outright, and let him take it away with him. Go, then, within the house and busy yourself with your daily duties, your loom, your distaff, and the ordering of your servants. This bow is a man's matter, and mine above all others, for it is I who am master here."

She went wondering back into the house, and laid her son's saying in her heart. Then

---

1　Elis 是古希腊城邦。

going upstairs with her handmaids into her room, she mourned her dear husband till Minerva sent sweet sleep over her eyelids.

The swineherd now took up the bow and was for taking it to Ulysses, but the suitors clamoured at him from all parts of the cloisters, and one of them said, "You idiot, where are you taking the bow to? Are you out of your wits? If Apollo and the other gods will grant our prayer, your own boarhounds shall get you into some quiet little place, and worry you to death."

Eumaeus[1] was frightened at the outcry they all raised, so he put the bow down then and there, but Telemachus shouted out at him from the other side of the cloisters, and threatened him saying, "Father Eumaeus, bring the bow on in spite of them, or young as I am I will pelt you with stones back to the country, for I am the better man of the two. I wish I was as much stronger than all the other suitors in the house as I am than you, I would soon send some of them off sick and sorry, for they mean mischief."

Thus did he speak, and they all of them laughed heartily, which put them in a better humour with Telemachus; so Eumaeus brought the bow on and placed it in the hands of Ulysses. When he had done this, he called Euryclea apart and said to her, "Euryclea, Telemachus says you are to close the doors of the women's apartments. If they hear any groaning or uproar as of men fighting about the house, they are not to come out, but are to keep quiet and stay where they are at their work."

Euryclea did as she was told and closed the doors of the women's apartments.

Meanwhile Philoetius[2] slipped quietly out and made fast the gates of the outer court. ... Ulysses... had now got the bow in his hands, and was turning it every way about, and proving it all over to see whether the worms had been eating into its two horns during his absence. Then would one turn towards his neighbour saying, "This is some tricky old bow-fancier; either he has got one like it at home, or he wants to make one, in such workmanlike style does the old vagabond handle it."

Another said, "I hope he may be no more successful in other things than he is likely to be in stringing this bow."

---

1 Eumaeus 是尤利西斯的牧猪奴。

2 Philoetius 是尤利西斯的牧牛奴。

But Ulysses, when he had taken it up and examined it all over, strung it as easily as a skilled bard strings a new peg of his lyre and makes the twisted gut fast at both ends. Then he took it in his right hand to prove the string, and it sang sweetly under his touch like the twittering of a swallow. The suitors were dismayed, and turned colour as they heard it; at that moment, moreover, Jove thundered loudly as a sign, and the heart of Ulysses rejoiced as he heard the omen that the son of scheming Saturn had sent him.

He took an arrow that was lying upon the table—for those which the Achaeans were so shortly about to taste were all inside the quiver—he laid it on the centre-piece of the bow, and drew the notch of the arrow and the string toward him, still seated on his seat. When he had taken aim he let fly, and his arrow pierced every one of the handle-holes of the axes from the first onwards till it had gone right through them, and into the outer courtyard. Then he said to Telemachus:

"Your guest has not disgraced you, Telemachus. I did not miss what I aimed at, and I was not long in stringing my bow. I am still strong, and not as the suitors twit me with being. Now, however, it is time for the Achaeans to prepare supper while there is still daylight, and then otherwise to disport themselves with song and dance which are the crowning ornaments of a banquet."

As he spoke he made a sign with his eyebrows, and Telemachus girded on his sword, grasped his spear, and stood armed beside his father's seat.

(From Book XXI)

Then Ulysses tore off his rags, and sprang on to the broad pavement with his bow and his quiver full of arrows. He shed the arrows on to the ground at his feet and said, "The mighty contest is at an end. I will now see whether Apollo will vouchsafe it to me to hit another mark which no man has yet hit."

On this he aimed a deadly arrow at Antinous, who was about to take up a two-handled gold cup to drink his wine and already had it in his hands. He had no thought of death—who amongst all the revellers would think that one man, however brave, would stand alone among so many and kill him? The arrow struck Antinous in the throat, and the point went clean through his neck, so that he fell over and the cup dropped from his hand, while a thick stream of blood gushed from his nostrils. He kicked the table from him and upset the things on it, so that the bread and roasted meats were all soiled as they fell over on to the ground. The suitors were in an uproar when they saw that a man had been hit; they sprang in dismay one and all of them from their seats and looked everywhere towards the walls, but there was neither shield nor spear, and they rebuked Ulysses very angrily. "Stranger," said they, "you shall pay for shooting people in this way: you shall see no other contest; you are a doomed man; he whom you have slain was the foremost youth in Ithaca, and the vultures shall devour you for having killed him."

Thus they spoke, for they thought that he had killed Antinous by mistake, and did not perceive that death was hanging over the head of every one of them. But Ulysses glared at them and said:

"Dogs, did you think that I should not come back from Troy? You have wasted my substance, have forced my women servants to lie with you, and have wooed my wife while I was still living. You have feared neither God nor man, and now you shall die."

They turned pale with fear as he spoke, and every man looked round about to see whither he might fly for safety, but Eurymachus alone spoke.

"If you are Ulysses," said he, "then what you have said is just. We have done much wrong on your lands and in your house. But Antinous who was the head and front of the offending lies low already. It was all his doing. It was not that he wanted to marry Penelope; he did not so much care about that; what he wanted was something quite different, and Jove has not vouchsafed it to him; he wanted to kill your son and to be chief man in Ithaca. Now, therefore, that he has met the death which was his due, spare the lives of your people. We will make everything good among ourselves, and pay you in full for all that we have eaten and drunk. Each one of us shall pay you a fine worth twenty oxen, and we will keep on giving you gold and bronze till your heart is softened. Until we have done this no one can complain of your being enraged against us."

Ulysses again glared at him and said, "Though you should give me all that you have in the world both now and all that you ever shall have, I will not stay my hand till I have paid all of you in full. You must fight, or fly for your lives; and fly, not a man of you shall."

Their hearts sank as they heard him, but Eurymachus again spoke saying:

"My friends, this man will give us no quarter. He will stand where he is and shoot us down till he has killed every man among us. Let us then show fight; draw your swords, and hold up the tables to shield you from his arrows. Let us have at him with a rush, to drive him from the pavement and doorway: we can then get through into the town, and raise such an alarm as shall soon stay his shooting."

As he spoke he drew his keen blade of bronze, sharpened on both sides, and with a loud cry sprang towards Ulysses, but Ulysses instantly shot an arrow into his breast that caught him by the nipple and fixed itself in his liver. He dropped his sword and fell doubled up over his table. The cup and all the meats went over on to the ground as he smote the earth with his forehead in the agonies of death, and he kicked the stool with his feet until his eyes were closed in darkness.

...

...Then Jove's daughter Minerva came up to them, having assumed the voice and form of Mentor. Ulysses was glad when he saw her and said, "Mentor, lend me your help, and forget not your old comrade, nor the many good turns he has done you. Besides, you are my age-mate."

But all the time he felt sure it was Minerva, and the suitors from the other side raised an uproar when they saw her. Agelaus was the first to reproach her. "Mentor," he cried, "do not let Ulysses beguile you into siding with him and fighting the suitors. This is what we will do: when we have killed these people, father and son, we will kill you too. You shall pay for it with your head, and when we have killed you, we will take all you have, in doors or out, and bring it into hotch-pot with Ulysses' property; we will not let your sons live in your house, nor your daughters, nor shall your widow continue to live in the city of Ithaca."

This made Minerva still more furious, so she scolded Ulysses very angrily. "Ulysses," said she, "your strength and prowess are no longer what they were when you fought for nine long years among the Trojans about the noble lady Helen. You killed many a man in those days, and it was through your stratagem that Priam's city was taken. How comes it that you are so lamentably less valiant now that you are on your own ground, face to face with the suitors in your own house? Come on, my good fellow, stand by my side and see how Mentor, son of Alcimus shall fight your foes and requite your kindnesses conferred upon him."

But she would not give him full victory as yet, for she wished still further to prove his own prowess and that of his brave son, so she flew up to one of the rafters in the roof of the cloister and sat upon it in the form of a swallow.

Meanwhile Agelaus son of Damastor, Eurynomus, Amphimedon, Demoptolemus, Pisander, and Polybus son of Polyctor bore the brunt of the fight upon the suitors' side; of all those who were still fighting for their lives they were by far the most valiant, for the others had already fallen under the arrows of Ulysses. Agelaus shouted to them and said, "My friends, he will soon have to leave off, for Mentor has gone away after having done nothing for him but brag. They are standing at the doors unsupported. Do not aim at him all at once, but six of you throw your spears first, and see if you cannot cover yourselves with glory by killing him. When he has fallen we need not be uneasy about the others."

They threw their spears as he bade them, but Minerva made them all of no effect. One hit the door post; another went against the door; the pointed shaft of another struck the wall; and as soon as they had avoided all the spears of the suitors Ulysses said to his own men, "My friends, I should say we too had better let drive into the middle of them, or they will crown all the harm they have done us by killing us outright."

They therefore aimed straight in front of them and threw their spears. Ulysses killed Demoptolemus, Telemachus Euryades, Eumaeus Elatus, while the stockman killed Pisander. These all bit the dust, and as the others drew back into a corner Ulysses and his men rushed forward and regained their spears by drawing them from the bodies of the dead.

...

...Ulysses struck the son of Damastor with a spear in close fight, while Telemachus hit Leocritus son of Evenor in the belly, and the dart went clean through him, so that he fell forward full on his face upon the ground. Then Minerva from her seat on the rafter held up her deadly aegis, and the hearts of the suitors quailed. They fled to the other end of the court like a herd of cattle maddened by the gadfly in early summer when the days are at their longest. As eagle-beaked, crook-taloned vultures from the mountains swoop down on the smaller birds that cower in flocks upon the ground, and kill them, for they cannot either fight or fly, and lookers on enjoy the sport—even so did Ulysses and his men fall upon the suitors and smite them on every side. They made a horrible groaning as their brains were being battered in, and the ground seethed with their blood.

Leiodes then caught the knees of Ulysses and said, "Ulysses I beseech you have mercy upon me and spare me. I never wronged any of the women in your house either in word or deed, and I tried to stop the others. I saw them, but they would not listen, and now they are paying for their folly. I was their sacrificing priest; if you kill me, I shall die without having done anything to deserve it, and shall have got no thanks for all the good that I did."

Ulysses looked sternly at him and answered, "If you were their sacrificing priest, you must have prayed many a time that it might be long before I got home again, and that you might marry my wife and have children by her. Therefore you shall die."

With these words he picked up the sword that Agelaus had dropped when he was being killed, and which was lying upon the ground. Then he struck Leiodes on the back of his neck, so that his head fell rolling in the dust while he was yet speaking.

The minstrel Phemius son of Terpes—he who had been forced by the suitors to sing to them—now tried to save his life. He was standing near towards the trap door, and held his lyre in his hand. He did not know whether to fly out of the cloister and sit down by the altar of Jove that was in the outer court, and on which both Laertes and Ulysses had offered up the thigh bones of many an ox, or whether to go straight up to Ulysses and embrace his knees, but in the end he deemed it best to embrace Ulysses' knees. So he laid his lyre on the ground between the mixing bowl and the silver-studded seat; then going up to Ulysses he caught hold of his knees and said, "Ulysses, I beseech you have mercy on me and spare me. You will be sorry for it afterwards if you kill a bard who can sing both for gods and men as I can. I make all my lays myself, and heaven visits me with every kind of inspiration. I would sing to you as though you were a god, do not therefore be in such a hurry to cut my head off. Your own son Telemachus will tell you that I did not want to frequent your house and sing to the suitors after their meals, but they were too many and too strong for me, so they made me."

Telemachus heard him, and at once went up to his father. "Hold!" he cried, "the man is guiltless, do him no hurt; and we will spare Medon[1] too, who was always good to me when I was a boy, unless Philoetius or Eumaeus has already killed him, or he has fallen in your way when you were raging about the court."

Medon caught these words of Telemachus, for he was crouching under a seat beneath which he had hidden by covering himself up with a freshly flayed heifer's hide, so he threw off the hide, went up to Telemachus, and laid hold of his knees.

1　Medon 是传令官。

"Here I am, my dear sir," said he, "stay your hand therefore, and tell your father, or he will kill me in his rage against the suitors for having wasted his substance and been so foolishly disrespectful to yourself."

Ulysses smiled at him and answered, "Fear not; Telemachus has saved your life, that you may know in future, and tell other people, how greatly better good deeds prosper than evil ones. Go, therefore, outside the cloisters into the outer court, and be out of the way of the slaughter—you and the bard—while I finish my work here inside."

The pair went into the outer court as fast as they could, and sat down by Jove's great altar, looking fearfully round, and still expecting that they would be killed. Then Ulysses searched the whole court carefully over, to see if anyone had managed to hide himself and was still living, but he found them all lying in the dust and weltering in their blood. They were like fishes which fishermen have netted out of the sea, and thrown upon the beach to lie gasping for water till the heat of the sun makes an end of them. Even so were the suitors lying all huddled up one against the other.

(From Book XXII)

思考题

QUESTIONS

1 Does Penelope know that none of the suitors is able to string Ulysses' bow when she sets up the contest?

2 What quality does Ulysses show when he strings the bow and shoots through the twelve axes?

3 What is Penelope holding to hide her face when she appears before the suitors?

4 It is the direst death slain at banquet. This is how Agamemnon dies in Chapter 8, which serves as a foil to Ulysses' fate. How does the fate of Ulysses form a contrast to that of Agamemnon?

5 Ulysses spares the bard after killing all the suitors. Does he hold the same attitude toward the bard with the Phaeacians?

6 What is the suitors' real purpose for wooing Penelope?

7 Telemachus orders his mother to go back to her place and leave the bow contest to men. Read it in contrast to a similar plot in Chapter 1 (Page 10) where the same wording is used, and tell what role Telemachus is trying to assume in either case.

8 When Ulysses and Telemachus are slaying the suitors, women remain within the doors of women's apartments. What can you tell about the household layout in Greece? What does the layout reveal about men's and women's activities?

第十二章

婚床揭秘
破镜重圆

导
读

INTRODUCTION

　　本章选自《奥德赛》第二十三卷。在杀戮求婚人、血洗厅堂之后，尤利西斯来到佩涅洛佩身边，向妻子表明了身份。但佩涅洛佩并不相信他的话，她假意提出要搬动婚床，实则在试探尤利西斯的真假。尤利西斯情急之下说出了婚床无法挪动的秘密，这个秘密只有他们夫妻二人知道，他也因此证实了自己的身份。此后夫妻相认，共叙别情。在史诗中尤利西斯素以狡狯著称，但在本卷中他却在聪慧的妻子前落了下风。

　　尤利西斯历经艰险、漂泊十年才返回家园，回到家中却不得不掩藏身份，而当他表明真实身份的时候，他最亲近的妻子却不相信他。尤利西斯在史诗中曾在众多场合表明过身份，这是唯一一次不被相信。佩涅洛佩对尤利西斯的试探，表明她在智谋上足以与夫君相匹敌。历尽劫波，二人终于团圆。夫妻相认后相拥夜话。这一段篇幅虽然不长，却是整部史诗中最平静温馨的部分。

选文

SELECTION

Euryclea now went upstairs laughing to tell her mistress that her dear husband had come home. Her aged knees became young again and her feet were nimble for joy as she went up to her mistress and bent over her head to speak to her. "Wake up Penelope, my dear child," she exclaimed, "and see with your own eyes something that you have been wanting this long time past. Ulysses has at last indeed come home again, and has killed the suitors who were giving so much trouble in his house, eating up his estate and ill treating his son."

"My good nurse," answered Penelope, "you must be mad. The gods sometimes send some very sensible people out of their minds, and make foolish people become sensible. This is what they must have been doing to you; for you always used to be a reasonable person. Why should you thus mock me when I have trouble enough already—talking such nonsense, and waking me up out of a sweet sleep that had taken possession of my eyes and closed them? I have never slept so soundly from the day my poor husband went to that city with the ill-omened name. Go back again into the women's room; if it had been any one else who had woke me up to bring me such absurd news I should have sent her away with a severe scolding. As it is your age shall protect you."

"My dear child," answered Euryclea, "I am not mocking you. It is quite true as I tell you that Ulysses is come home again. He was the stranger whom they all kept on treating so badly in the cloister. Telemachus knew all the time that he was come back, but kept his father's secret that he might have his revenge on all these wicked people."

Then Penelope sprang up from her couch, threw her arms round Euryclea, and wept for joy. "But my dear nurse," said she, "explain this to me; if he has really come home as you say, how did he manage to overcome the wicked suitors single handed, seeing what a number of them there always were?"

"I was not there," answered Euryclea, "and do not know; I only heard them groaning while they were being killed. We sat crouching and huddled up in a corner of the women's room with the doors closed, till your son came to fetch me because his father sent him. Then I found Ulysses standing over the corpses that were lying on the ground all round him, one on top of the other. You would have enjoyed it if you could have seen him standing there all bespattered with blood and filth, and looking just like a lion. But the corpses are now all piled up in the gatehouse that is in the outer court, and Ulysses has lit a great fire to purify the house with sulphur. He has sent me to call you, so come with me that you may both be happy together after all; for now at last the desire of your heart has been fulfilled; your husband is come home to find both wife and son alive and well, and to take his revenge in his own house on the suitors who behaved so badly to him."

"My dear nurse," said Penelope, "do not exult too confidently over all this. You know how delighted every one would be to see Ulysses come home—more particularly myself, and the son who has been born to both of us; but what you tell me cannot be really true. It is some god who is angry with the suitors for their great wickedness, and has made an end of them; for they respected no man in the whole world, neither rich nor poor, who came near them, and they have come to a bad end in consequence of their iniquity; Ulysses is dead far away from the Achaean land; he will never return home again."

Then nurse Euryclea said, "My child, what are you talking about? But you were all hard of belief and have made up your mind that your husband is never coming, although he is in the house and by his own fire side at this very moment. Besides I can give you another proof; when I was washing him I perceived the scar which the wild boar gave him, and I wanted to tell you about it, but in his wisdom he would not let me, and clapped his hands over my mouth; so come with me and I will make this bargain with you—if I am deceiving you, you may have me killed by the most cruel death you can think of."

"My dear nurse," said Penelope, "however wise you may be you can hardly fathom the counsels of the gods. Nevertheless, we will go in search of my son, that I may see the corpses of the suitors, and the man who has killed them."

On this she came down from her upper room, and while doing so she considered whether she should keep at a distance from her husband and question him, or whether she should at once go up to him and embrace him. When, however, she had crossed the stone floor of the cloister, she sat down opposite Ulysses by the fire, against the wall at right angles [to that by which she had entered], while Ulysses sat near one of the bearing-posts, looking upon the ground, and waiting to see what his brave wife would say to him when she saw him. For a long time she sat silent and as one lost in amazement. At one moment she looked him full in the face, but then again directly, she was misled by his shabby clothes and failed to recognise him, till Telemachus began to reproach her and said:

"Mother—but you are so hard that I cannot call you by such a name—why do you keep away from my father in this way? Why do you not sit by his side and begin talking to him and asking him questions? No other woman could bear to keep away from her husband when he had come back to her after twenty years of absence, and after having gone through so much; but your heart always was as hard as a stone."

Penelope answered, "My son, I am so lost in astonishment that I can find no words in which either to ask questions or to answer them. I cannot even look him straight in the face. Still, if he really is Ulysses come back to his own home again, we shall get to understand one another better by and by, for there are tokens with which we two are alone acquainted, and which are hidden from all others."

Ulysses smiled at this, and said to Telemachus, "Let your mother put me to any proof she likes; she will make up her mind about it presently. She rejects me for the moment and believes me to be somebody else, because I am covered with dirt and have such bad clothes on; let us, however, consider what we had better do next. When one man has killed another—even though he was not one who would leave many friends to take up his quarrel—the man who has killed him must still say good bye to his friends and fly the country; whereas we have been killing the stay of a whole town, and all the picked youth of Ithaca. I would have you consider this matter."

"Look to it yourself, father," answered Telemachus, "for they say you are the wisest counsellor in the world, and that there is no other mortal man who can compare with you. We will follow you with right good will, nor shall you find us fail you in so far as our strength holds out."

"I will say what I think will be best," answered Ulysses. "First wash and put your shirts on; tell the maids also to go to their own room and dress; Phemius shall then strike up a dance tune on his lyre, so that if people outside hear, or any of the neighbours, or some one going along the street happens to notice it, they may think there is a wedding in the house, and no rumours about the death of the suitors will get about in the town, before we can escape to the woods upon my own land. Once there, we will settle which of the courses heaven vouchsafes us shall seem wisest."

Thus did he speak, and they did even as he had said. First they washed and put their shirts on, while the women got ready. Then Phemius took his lyre and set them all longing for sweet song and stately dance. The house re-echoed with the sound of men and women dancing, and the people outside said, "I suppose the queen has been getting married at last. She ought to be ashamed of herself for not continuing to protect her husband's property until he comes home."

This was what they said, but they did not know what it was that had been happening. The upper servant Eurynome washed and anointed Ulysses in his own house and gave him a shirt and cloak, while Minerva made him look taller and stronger than before; she also made the hair grow thick on the top of his head, and flow down in curls like hyacinth blossoms; she glorified him about the head and shoulders just as a skilful workman who has studied art of all kinds under Vulcan or Minerva—and his work is full of beauty—enriches a piece of silver plate by gilding it. He came from the bath looking like one of the immortals, and sat down opposite his wife on the seat he had left. "My dear," said he, "heaven has endowed you with a heart more unyielding than woman ever yet had. No other woman could bear to keep away from her husband when he had come back to her after twenty years of absence, and after having gone through so much. But come, nurse, get a bed ready for me; I will sleep alone, for this woman has a heart as hard as iron."

"My dear," answered Penelope, "I have no wish to set myself up, nor to depreciate you; but I am not struck by your appearance, for I very well remember what kind of a man you were when you set sail from Ithaca. Nevertheless, Euryclea, take his bed outside the bed chamber that he himself built. Bring the bed outside this room, and put bedding upon it with fleeces, good coverlets, and blankets."

She said this to try him, but Ulysses was very angry and said, "Wife, I am much displeased at what you have just been saying. Who has been taking my bed from the place in which I left it? He must have found it a hard task, no matter how skilled a workman he was, unless some god came and helped him to shift it. There is no man living, however strong and in his prime, who could move it from its place, for it is a marvellous curiosity which I made with my very own hands. There was a young olive growing within the precincts of the house, in full vigour, and about as thick as a bearing-post. I built my room round this with strong walls of stone and a roof to cover them, and I made the doors strong and well-fitting. Then I cut off the top boughs of the olive tree and left the stump standing. This I dressed roughly from the root upwards and then worked with carpenter's tools well and skillfully, straightening my work by drawing a line on the wood, and making it into a bed-prop. I then bored a hole down the middle, and made it the centre-post of my bed, at which I worked till I had finished it, inlaying it with gold and silver; after this I stretched a hide of crimson leather from one side of it to the other. So you see I know all about it, and I desire to learn whether it is still there, or whether any one has been removing it by cutting down the olive tree at its roots."

When she heard the sure proofs Ulysses now gave her, she fairly broke down. She flew weeping to his side, flung her arms about his neck, and kissed him. "Do not be angry with me Ulysses," she cried, "you, who are the wisest of mankind. We have suffered, both of us. Heaven has denied us the happiness of spending our youth, and of growing old, together; do not then be aggrieved or take it amiss that I did not embrace you thus as soon as I saw you. I have been shuddering all the time through fear that someone might come here and deceive me with a lying story; for there are many very wicked people going about. Jove's daughter Helen would never have yielded herself to a man from a foreign country, if she had known that the sons of Achaeans would come after her and bring her back. Heaven put it in her heart to do wrong, and she gave no thought to that sin, which has been the source of all our sorrows. Now, however, that you have convinced me by showing that you know all about our bed (which no human being has ever seen but you and I and a single maidservant, the daughter of Actor, who was given me by my father on my marriage, and who keeps the doors of our room) hard of belief though I have been I can mistrust no longer."

Then Ulysses in his turn melted, and wept as he clasped his dear and faithful wife to his bosom. As the sight of land is welcome to men who are swimming towards the shore, when Neptune has wrecked their ship with the fury of his winds and waves; a few alone reach the land, and these, covered with brine, are thankful when they find themselves on firm ground and out of danger—even so was her husband welcome to her as she looked upon him, and she could not tear her two fair arms from about his neck. Indeed they would have gone on indulging their sorrow till rosy-fingered morn appeared, had not Minerva determined otherwise, and held night back in the far west, while she would not suffer Dawn to leave Oceanus, nor to yoke the two steeds Lampus and Phaethon that bear her onward to break the day upon mankind.

At last, however, Ulysses said, "Wife, we have not yet reached the end of our troubles. I have an unknown amount of toil still to undergo. It is long and difficult, but I must go through with it, for thus the shade of Teiresias prophesied concerning me, on the day when I went down into Hades to ask about my return and that of my companions. But now let us go to bed, that we may lie down and enjoy the blessed boon of sleep."

"You shall go to bed as soon as you please," replied Penelope, "now that the gods have sent you home to your own good house and to your country. But as heaven has put it in your mind to speak of it, tell me about the task that lies before you. I shall have to hear about it later, so it is better that I should be told at once."

"My dear," answered Ulysses, "why should you press me to tell you? Still, I will not conceal it from you, though you will not like it. I do not like it myself, for Teiresias bade me travel far and wide, carrying an oar, till I came to a country where the people have never heard of the sea, and do not even mix salt with their food. They know nothing about ships, nor oars that are as the wings of a ship. He gave me this certain token which I will not hide from you. He said that a wayfarer should meet me and ask me whether it was a winnowing shovel that I had on my shoulder. On this, I was to fix my oar in the ground and sacrifice a ram, a bull, and a boar to Neptune; after which I was to go home and offer hecatombs to all the gods in heaven, one after the other. As for myself, he said that death should come to me from the sea, and that my life should ebb away very gently when I was full of years and peace of mind, and my people should bless me. All this, he said, should surely come to pass."

And Penelope said, "If the gods are going to vouchsafe you a happier time in your old age, you may hope then to have some respite from misfortune." Thus did they converse. Meanwhile Eurynome and the nurse took torches and made the bed ready with soft coverlets; as soon as they had laid them, the nurse went back into the house to go to her rest, leaving the bed chamber woman Eurynome to show Ulysses and Penelope to bed by torch light. When she had conducted them to their room she went back, and they then came joyfully to the rites of their own old bed. Telemachus, Philoetius, and the swineherd now left off dancing, and made the women leave off also. They then laid themselves down to sleep in the cloisters.

When Ulysses and Penelope had had their fill of love they fell talking with one another. She told him how much she had had to bear in seeing the house filled with a crowd of wicked suitors who had killed so many sheep and oxen on her account, and had drunk so many casks of wine. Ulysses in his turn told her what he had suffered, and how much trouble he had himself given to other people. He told her everything, and she was so delighted to listen that she never went to sleep till he had ended his whole story.

He began with his victory over the Cicons, and how he thence reached the fertile land of the Lotus-eaters. He told her all about the Cyclops and how he had punished him for having so ruthlessly eaten his brave comrades; how he then went on to Aeolus, who received him hospitably and furthered him on his way, but even so he was not to reach home, for to his great grief a hurricane carried him out to sea again; how he went on to the Laestrygonian city Telepylos, where the people destroyed all his ships with their crews, save himself and his own ship only. Then he told of cunning Circe and her craft, and how he sailed to the chill house of Hades, to consult the ghost of the Theban prophet Teiresias, and how he saw his old comrades in arms, and his mother who bore him and brought him up when he was a child; how he then heard the wondrous singing of the Sirens, and went on to the wandering rocks and terrible Charybdis and to Scylla, whom no man had ever yet passed in safety; how his men then ate the cattle of the sun-god, and how Jove therefore struck the ship with his thunderbolts, so that all his men perished together, himself alone being left alive; how at last he reached the Ogygian island and the nymph Calypso, who kept him there in a cave, and fed him, and wanted him to marry her, in which case she intended making him immortal so that he should never grow old, but she could not persuade him to let her do so; and how after much suffering he had found his way to the Phaeacians, who had treated him as though he had been a god, and sent him back in a ship to his own country after having given him gold, bronze, and raiment in great abundance. This was the last thing about which he told her, for here a deep sleep took hold upon him and eased the burden of his sorrows.

...

(From Book XXIII)

思考题

QUESTIONS

1. When Euryclea tells Penelope Ulysses has come back, what is Penelope's response?

2. Is the death of the suitors the end of the epic? What does Ulysses plan to do to prevent the rumors about the death of the suitors?

3. Seen from people's words (Page 154), would it be acceptable if Penelope remarried?

4. What is the secret that only Ulysses and Penelope know?

5. How does Penelope try Ulysses? Why do you think she can succeed?

6. The most serene and harmonious moment in the epic is when Ulysses and Penelope talk in bed. What might be the couple's feelings when they tell each other their experiences?

7. What is the fate of Ulysses prophesied by Teiresias?

8. Inspired by the description about the prophesied future of Ulysses, Alfred Tennyson writes a poem entitled "Ulysses". Read the poem on the next page and see what the hero is like in the poem. What is the poet's understanding of the hero? Does Tennyson's "Ulysses" hold the same values with Homer's "Ulysses"?

Ulysses

By Alfred Tennyson

It little profits that an idle king,

By this still hearth, among these barren crags,

Match'd with an aged wife, I mete and dole

Unequal laws unto a savage race,

That hoard, and sleep, and feed, and know not me.

I cannot rest from travel: I will drink

Life to the lees; all times I have enjoy'd

Greatly, have suffer'd greatly, both with those

That loved me, and alone; on shore, and when

Thro' scudding drifts the rainy Hyades

Vext the dim sea: I am become a name;

For always roaming with a hungry heart

Much have I seen and known; cities of men

And manners, climates, councils, governments,

Myself not least, but honour'd of them all;

And drunk delight of battle with my peers,

Far on the ringing plains of windy Troy,

I am a part of all that I have met;

Yet all experience is an arch wherethro'

Gleams that untravell'd world, whose margin fades

For ever and for ever when I move.

How dull it is to pause, to make an end,

To rust unburnish'd, not to shine in use!

As tho' to breathe were life. Life piled on life

Were all too little, and of one to me

Little remains: but every hour is saved

From that eternal silence, something more,

A bringer of new things; and vile it were

For some three suns to store and hoard myself,

And this gray spirit yearning in desire

To follow knowledge like a sinking star,

Beyond the utmost bound of human thought.

This is my son, mine own Telemachus,

To whom I leave the scepter and the isle—

Well-loved of me, discerning to fulfil

This labour, by slow prudence to make mild

A rugged people, and thro' soft degrees

Subdue them to the useful and the good.

Most blameless is he, centred in the sphere

Of common duties, decent not to fail

In offices of tenderness, and pay

Meet adoration to my household gods,

When I am gone. He works his work, I mine.

There lies the port; the vessel puffs her sail:

There gloom the dark broad seas. My mariners,

Souls that have toil'd, and wrought, and thought with me—

That ever with a frolic welcome took

The thunder and the sunshine, and opposed

Free hearts, free foreheads—you and I are old;

Old age hath yet his honour and his toil;

Death closes all: but something ere the end,

Some work of noble note, may yet be done,

Not unbecoming men that strove with Gods.

The lights begin to twinkle from the rocks:

The long day wanes: the slow moon climbs: the deep

Moans round with many voices. Come, my friends,

'Tis not too late to seek a newer world.

Push off, and sitting well in order smite

The sounding furrows; for my purpose holds

To sail beyond the sunset, and the baths

Of all the western stars, until I die.

It may be that the gulfs will wash us down:

It may be we shall touch the Happy Isles,

And see the great Achilles, whom we knew.

Tho' much is taken, much abides; and tho'

We are not now that strength which in old days

Moved earth and heaven; that which we are, we are;

One equal temper of heroic hearts,

Made weak by time and fate, but strong in will

To strive, to seek, to find, and not to yield.